The Amish Veronica Series #3

I0629370

Merry Amish Christmas

Stephanie Schwartz

Medical Disclaimer

This book is not intended as a substitute for the medical advice of your midwife, obstetrician, physician, pediatrician, or other care providers, but rather is meant to supplement, not replace your primary health care person (s). The reader should regularly consult with one of the above care providers in matters relating to his/her health or your baby's health, particularly with respect to any symptoms that may require diagnosis or medical attention. This book has incorporated "Best Practice" guidelines as much as possible and encourages all parents to continue to research the subjects discussed here as new studies are continually being done both here in the U.S. and abroad.

Clarification here

Since I often refer to a mother as 'she' or 'her,' I call most babies in my stories 'he' or 'him,' though I love baby girls just as much and will take any you don't want. Really.

If you find mistakes...

In this or any of my books, please consider that they are there for a purpose. I try to write something for everyone, and some people are always looking for mistakes.

The Glossary*

Abbeditlich – Pennsylvania Dutch dialect word meaning "delicious."

Ach! – Plain expression meaning "Oh!"

Aendi – Pennsylvania Dutch dialect word meaning "auntie." (familiar)

Amische – Pennsylvania Dutch dialect word meaning "The Amish."

Erschtaunlich – Pennsylvania Dutch dialect word meaning "astonishing."

Baremlich – Pennsylvania Dutch dialect word meaning "terrible/horrible."

Bebottsdaag – Pennsylvania Dutch dialect word meaning "birthday."

Beheef dich – Pennsylvania Dutch dialect expression meaning "Behave, you."

Bief – Pennsylvania Dutch dialect word meaning "pie."

Bobbel – Pennsylvania Dutch dialect word meaning "baby" singular.

Bobbeli – Pennsylvania Dutch dialect word meaning "babies" plural.

Brau – Pennsylvania Dutch dialect word meaning "pray."

Bredder – Pennsylvania Dutch dialect word meaning "bread."

Bruder – Pennsylvania Dutch dialect word meaning "brother."

Brunne – Pennsylvania Dutch dialect word meaning "bunny."

Buwe – Pennsylvania Dutch dialect word meaning "boys."

Chust – Pennsylvania Dutch dialect word meaning "just."

Dat – Pennsylvania Dutch dialect word referring to or addressing one's "Dad, Father."

Darr – Pennsylvania Dutch dialect word meaning "dear."

Daumling – Pennsylvania Dutch dialect word meaning "darling."

Dawdi haus – Pennsylvania Dutch dialect word meaning "a grandparents' apartment usually attached to a main house."

Die gut shtup – Pennsylvania Dutch dialect word for "living room."

Denki – Pennsylvania Dutch dialect word meaning "thank you."

Dochder – Pennsylvania Dutch dialect word meaning "daughter."

Doddy – Pennsylvania Dutch dialect word meaning or when addressing one's "Grandfather."

Dunner uns Gewidder – Pennsylvania Dutch saying meaning "Confound it!"

Englische (rs) – Pennsylvania Dutch dialect general term meaning "non-Amish."

Erschtaunlich – Pennsylvania Dutch dialect general term meaning "astonishing."

Esschtick – Pennsylvania Dutch dialect word meaning "lunch."

Ferhoodled – Pennsylvania Dutch dialect word meaning "mixed up or new-fangled."

Frau(s) – Pennsylvania Dutch dialect word meaning "wife/wives, (plural)."

Friede – Pennsylvania Dutch dialect word meaning "friends."

Gaund – Pennsylvania Dutch dialect word meaning "dress."

Geblumpt – Pennsylvania Dutch dialect word meaning "plump."

Geendt – Pennsylvania Dutch dialect word meaning "eat."

Glieder – Pennsylvania Dutch dialect word meaning "kitten."

Gott – Pennsylvania Dutch dialect word meaning "God."

Grischtdaag – Pennsylvania Dutch dialect word meaning "Christmas."

Grischtdaagnacht – Pennsylvania Dutch dialect word meaning "Christmas Eve."

Grossmammi – Pennsylvania Dutch dialect word meaning or addressing one's "Grandmother."

Gut – Pennsylvania Dutch dialect word meaning "good."

Hallicher – Pennsylvania Dutch dialect word meaning "happy or merry" as in greeting.

Halsband – Pennsylvania Dutch dialect word meaning "husband."

Hard – Pennsylvania Dutch dialect word meaning "heart."

Haus – Pennsylvania Dutch dialect word meaning "house."

Hinklehaus – Pennsylvania Dutch dialect word meaning "chicken coop."

Huddlich – Pennsylvania Dutch dialect word meaning "a mess."

Insch – Pennsylvania Dutch dialect word meaning "insane."

Joyeux Noël – French expression meaning "Merry Christmas."

Kaffi – Pennsylvania Dutch dialect word meaning "coffee."

Kapp – Pennsylvania Dutch dialect word meaning "prayer cap/bonnet."

Kavli – Pennsylvania Dutch dialect word meaning "Amish double-handled diaper basket/tote."

Kesselhaus – Pennsylvania Dutch dialect word meaning "wash house."

Kinner – Pennsylvania Dutch dialect word meaning "children."

Ks! – Pennsylvania Dutch dialect word meaning "Go!"

Kumm – Pennsylvania Dutch dialect word meaning "come."

Liebling – Pennsylvania Dutch dialect word meaning "darling."

Mariye-esse — Pennsylvania Dutch dialect word meaning "breakfast."

Mamm – Pennsylvania Dutch dialect word meaning "mother," or "Mom."

Mammi – Pennsylvania Dutch dialect word meaning "Grandma" (familiar.)

Maud – Pennsylvania Dutch dialect word meaning "maid," often hired.

Meedel – Pennsylvania Dutch dialect word meaning "little girl(s)."

Mosch – Pennsylvania Dutch word meaning "mush" as in hot cornmeal cereal.

Nacht – Pennsylvania Dutch word meaning "night."

Onkel – Pennsylvania Dutch dialect word meaning "uncle."

Patties down – Pennsylvania Dutch expression meaning "hands folded under the table on laps in preparation for grace."

Pennsylfaani – Pennsylvania Dutch dialect word for "Pennsylvania Dutch language."

Rapple – Pennsylvania Dutch dialect word for "rabbit."

Redd – Pennsylvania Dutch dialect word meaning "ready."

Schlaf gut – German/Plain meaning a warm, caring way to wish someone a good night's sleep.

Schlechdi! – Pennsylvania Dutch dialect word meaning "bad girl!"

Schmart – Pennsylvania Dutch dialect word meaning "smart."

Schnitz – Pennsylvania Dutch dialect word meaning "dried apples."

Schooss – Pennsylvania Dutch dialect word meaning "school."

Schtruvvels – Pennsylvania Dutch dialect word meaning "stray hairs."

Schwanger – Pennsylvania Dutch dialect word meaning "pregnant."

Shmuzzling – Pennsylvania Dutch dialect word meaning "hugging and kissing."

Sits ana – Pennsylvania Dutch expression meaning "(please) sit down."

Shlusss – Pennsylvania Dutch/German expression meaning "the end, done."

Tract – In Plain circles meaning "the standard dress."

Vorzaehle – Pennsylvania Dutch expression meaning "what is what? (going on?)"

Wunderbar-gut – Pennsylvania Dutch dialect word meaning "wonderful and good."

Ya – Pennsylvania Dutch dialect word meaning "yes" or "you."

Yesus – Pennsylvania Dutch dialect word for "Jesus."

Youngie – Pennsylvania Dutch dialect word meaning "the youth."

Yucke – Pennsylvania Dutch dialect word meaning "yuck."

Yunge – Pennsylvania Dutch dialect word meaning "junk, rubbish."

Zapper – Pennsylvania Dutch dialect word meaning "supper."

Ztvett Grischtdaag – Pennsylvania Dutch dialect name of "Second Christmas."

Ztzvilling – Pennsylvania Dutch dialect word meaning "twins."

Zum Mordsackerment! – Pennsylvania Dutch dialect expression used only in extreme circumstances meaning "hell and damnation!"

* Although I have tried to represent Pennsylvania Dutch and local dialects throughout my books as accurately as I can, I am sure my readers who are native speakers will always be able to find fault for which I sincerely ask forgiveness. I know I will never get it perfectly, but I hope you will allow for this. Thank you!

~ Stephanie

Recap from The Amish Veronica #2

YOU HAVE RAVISHED MY HEART

All her dreams had been dashed thus far. She survived those terrible turns of fate, but barely. She only wished to live out a simple life in her Amish community, seeking God, caring for a husband and a family, being part of a loving church. Are these things predestined for all eternity? Have the powers that be really brought him to her from so very far away? Can she trust God on this one? Was having faith meant to be this hard? But then, suddenly it appears that He really will wipe away every tear. Bringing Henry into her life changed absolutely everything. Her entire future as she imagined it, for one. And then Rose. Beyond her wildest dreams He has given her a daughter to love and cherish. Seemingly endless tragedy and sorrow, and then bliss and ecstasy. It is all too deep for words.

Part One

God Bless the master of this house,
Likewise, the mistress too,
And all the little children that round the table go.
And all your kin and kinsfolk that dwell both far and near,
May their barns be filled with wheat and corn,
and their hearts be always true,
To you a well-filled purse, a well-filled dish, too,
and a Merry [Amish] Christmas and a Happy New Year to you!

~ 1900s Carol from South England

CHAPTER 1

Kaffi Soup

"**M**amm! *MAMM!*" The shouting could be heard throughout the whole house.

"*Maaaaammm!*"

"What is it, for heaven's sake?" Veronica called back from the kitchen sink. She wasn't sure yet where it was coming from, but she had a good guess who it was. She could hear the old wooden stairs creaking as little feet bounded down them.

"Let's make *Dat* Shoo-fly *bief* for supper. Okay?" four-year-old-soon-to-be-five Rose called as she ran into the kitchen and stood barefoot in front of Veronica in her muslin nightie buttoned up to her chin, batting with her hands at her waist-length brown hairs covering one eye and most of the other one also.

"And corn noodle soup, too," she said from behind the curtain of hairs that she hadn't tamed yet. "Pleeeeeease," she begged then, her hands tightly clasped in front of her as if in prayer.

"Oh, my goodness, *daumling.* Your *Dat* will get absolutely *geblumpt* if we keep making him pies every day," she said.

"Oh, but we need to keep him happy, eh?" the little girl asked. "And you promised to teach me how to make it," she said, reminding Veronica of this fact that was as good as a binding legal contract in her little mind.

"Well, we'll see," Veronica said, taking in the little hands. "I have to make breakfast first. Then we'll see what we have to do today, that is if that meets with your highness' approval," Veronica explained.

"You have your chores before you eat, don't forget. Open their pen on the *hinklehaus* and scatter the chicken feed first. Then bring in all the eggs. There should be plenty today. Take your basket when you go. Go and get dressed and I'll do your hairs first," she added. With a nod of her head, and content that her prayer would be answered, the little sprite turned and was gone.

It had been six months since the wedding. My, but what a fine wedding it was, too. Maybe a bit grander than her first marriage even to Amos. Everyone was genuinely glad for Veronica and Henry, especially after all the hardship both had been through, first losing her tiny preemie baby and then Amos being killed in a buggy accident hardly a year later. That old guy driving the car was nearing his nineties, for goodness' sake. He never should have driven that big fancy car at all. He ran one stop sign. Just the one, but that's all it takes.

Henry had not escaped tragedy either. He and his young wife couldn't have been happier as they expected their first baby. No one could have imagined the complications that arose leading to her death. Little Rose survived the ordeal, though that seemed insignificant consolation to the bereft father.

Veronica had already been up for two hours. She was dressed in her favorite sage green *tract,* with her kitchen apron over that. She'd begun making a matching dress for Rose out of the same cotton-polyester cloth. Just enough polyester that she didn't have to iron it every time she washed it. Hanging on the clotheslines whipped all the wrinkles right out of it. It was also cooler in the summer months. The heavier fabrics were more suited for cold weather, worn over thermals or a wool slip.

Her white starched bonnet was already pinned in place over her tight, dark brown bun. She, too, was barefoot. Your feet toughen up when you only wear shoes for church or town trips. It also helps keep the floors clean if you aren't dragging in all sorts of dirt on your shoes every time you come into the house. You didn't worry as much about putting toddlers down to graze on the floors either. Hopefully the number of germs from the barns will be reduced there, too. Mind you, a certain amount of exposure to *some* germs builds up one's immunity to the environment.

The children loved being barefoot for the greater part of the year. If there wasn't frost on the ground, you'd find them barefoot, even in church or at school. There was the added benefit of saving literally tons of money on shoes for growing children. Stubbed toes and scraped knees were their lot no matter what they were or weren't wearing on their growing feet.

Veronica continued crumbling the day-old Southern Gal Biscuits into three bowls. Any bread would do. She saved all the crusts and heels of the bread in a bowl in the warming oven on the wood stove to dry out. There was so much you could do with old bread. Bread puddings, a binder for meatloaf, a fondu supper, breakfast *mosch*, a thickener for soups, herbie croutons for salads or Haystack suppers. The list went on. If you were out of bread or biscuits, you could always use crushed Saltine crackers for the breakfast kind. Homemade grapenuts would work too. Rose claimed that they should try popcorn in it sometime.

Veronica moved the scalded camel milk away from the hottest side of the wood stove. She measured out three tablespoons of instant coffee into the pan and stirred that into the hot milk, careful not to let it boil and burn. She stopped then, spoon frozen between the bowls and the coffee canister and closed her eyes to breathe in the rich coffee smell. Veronica loved this time of day. So silent, waiting for all the earth to awaken once again which it did every single day without fail. How did God do that, anyway? Would the ritual ever cease? In Eternity perhaps?

Looking back to what she'd been doing, she measured out three tablespoons of raw honey—brown sugar would do, too—stirred it in gently, and it was ready to pour over biscuits or bread or crackers. Adding a spritz of almond or vanilla extract or a dash of cinnamon is optional.

She had discovered camel milk only a couple of years ago. It is the perfect solution for those with lactose intolerance. An Amish fellow in Missouri has a herd of camels that he milks and sends it all over the country. A mama camel will only let down her milk if her calf is in the pen with her, Veronica had read.

The sun was just coming up and peeking into the kitchen windows. Veronica reached up above the table, cranked down the wick on the mantle lamp that was hanging from a chain in the beam above and blew the flame out.

Thriftiness is part of Amish culture. With large families we have learned to be frugal and to make the most out of the household items we have. Whether it's food, clothing, furniture, or bedding, Amish culture teaches a person not to be wasteful.
- Amish advice

CHAPTER 2

Who Hides the Eggs?

Rose would be starting school in the fall. Henry and Veronica decided recently to try speaking only English at home to help Rose make the transition to English easier. Amish children don't learn English as a second language until they attend school. Before that they only know *Pennsylfaani* or Pennsylvania Dutch.

Rose came back into the kitchen to have her hairs braided. Sitting at the kitchen table, swinging her legs that weren't long enough yet to touch the floor, she recited rhymes from her Mother Goose story book.

"The butcher, the baker, the candlestick maker..." as Veronica brushed and then braided her hairs. Then she rolled it all into a bun and secured it with stretchy bands. Her black cotton *kapp* tied under her chin completed the morning routine. Hopping off the chair she ran barefoot to the mud room and grabbed the egg basket hanging there. Then she stopped, spun around and ran back to the kitchen throwing her arms around Veronica's middle, the wire egg basket hitting her mother squarely at the back of her knees.

"So, what's that for?" Veronica laughed as she hugged Rose.

"*Chust* because I love you sooooo much, *Mamm,*" came her answer.

"Oh. I see. Well, I love you more," Veronica replied, hugging her back, wishing she didn't have to ever let her go.

"Oh, no you don't," Rose answered.

Then more subdued, she stood back a step and looked up at Veronica.

"Tell me about my first *mamm,* please?" she asked.

"Oh, well, then," Veronica began. "Get the eggs first and then let's sit down here for breakfast, *daumling.*"

"Okay," Rose agreed as she skipped toward the back door. Suddenly, Veronica called her back. "*Kumm* here, youse," she demanded.

"Huh?" Rose questioned, noticing the firmer voice this time. She froze in place.

"Would you please tell me, Missy," Veronica began, trying not to explode quite yet.

"What is that on your toenails?" she demanded.

"Well," Rose began cheerfully, aware that trouble could be brewing just now.

"Ya know last time we were at the farmers' market. Well, I saw all these ladies with painted toes *kumming* outta their sandals. So, I wanted to try that," she confidently stated.

"But what did you paint yours with? Why?" Veronica asked, no closer to understanding the little girl.

"I got the magic markers on *Dat's* desk," she explained, not too worried yet that this might spell consequences.

"Ya know, those are permanent, don't ya?" Veronica said, quite horrified at this point.

"But I thought they looked pretty." Rose figured this was a perfectly good explanation.

"Um, no." Veronica said, vigorously shaking her head.

"We don't paint ourselves or wear makeup or jewelry for a reason, my dear," Veronica answered, allowing for the child's innocence.

"*Gott* gave us our bodies to be His temples. We don't have to adorn ourselves. That's vanity. That's what the world does, *daumling,*" Veronica explained.

"All that makeup, jewelry and nail polish does is attract attention to us. That is a sin." Veronica had not imagined she'd be having this talk with her daughter this early. She was barely five, for pity's sake.

"Oh," was Rose's reply. She would have to understand this better. Perhaps later.

Henry had also been up early when he first heard Veronica puttering around the kitchen, pots clinking, the wood box on the old black iron cookstove being shaken to distribute the few hot coals there that had survived the night. Then he could hear a log being jiggled into place over the coals and the little door slamming shut on the wood box, and then the squeak of the rusty old damper being cranked open.

By the time Henry dressed, Veronica already had 'first breakfast' ready for him. A large tankard of strong coffee loaded with cream and sugar was the perfect thing to get you up and running on a brisk morning. He stood by the stove gulping the first swig of coffee. He'd carry the large mug with him toward the barn. Eyeing the empty cookie jar on the shelf above the stove, he was disappointed, wishing he could take along a handful with him on his way out. Seeing his eyes looking at the cookie jar, Veronica spoke up.

"So sorry it's empty," she stated. "We're hopefully making more later today."

"Maybe Monster cookies? Or your Dunkin' Snaps" he

suggested hopefully. Then he added, pushing his luck even further, "or both?" he asked meekly, looking over the top of his mug as he consoled himself with another large swig of coffee. His tousled curly brown hairs looked almost comical atop the lean face. He'd tried all during his teen years to get them to lay flat, even resorting to wearing an old stocking to bed after he'd wet it all down. It was a hopeless cause.

His clean shirt didn't hide his strong physique, his arms filling out the sleeves and his shoulders almost straining the fabric in back. Black leather suspenders were buttoned front and back at the waist of his barndoor trousers. Still barefoot, he took a step closer to Veronica. He leaned in, careful not to splash hot coffee on her, to plant a coffee-flavored kiss on her lips. Then he turned toward the door to put on his Wellington barn boots, these days called 'Wellies' for short. He slowed by the wood stove and reaching up to a peg there he grabbed his everyday wheat straw hat. It landed crooked on his head, but then the cows wouldn't care, would they?

"See ya soon," he called over his shoulder as he pushed open the door, his gray eyes twinkling with thoughts of all kinds of mischief. Then he winked at her. That was the one thing that always made her blush. Even after all these months. With that, the kitchen door banged shut with a thud and she returned to making a second breakfast which would happen when they were all at the table, the first chores done.

Almost two hours later, Henry was returning from the barn and his morning chores. He shook off his barn boots at the mud room's jute rug and hung up his straw hat on a peg on the wall, leaving his hairs plastered to his head with sweat.

He pulled up his barndoor trousers and tucked his shirt back down into his pants. His sleeves were already rolled up.

Walking to the chore sink by the door he opened the spigot on the gravity water tank and washed his hands with the fragrant homemade soap. Grabbing the towel below, he asked Veronica what was for breakfast. Then, as an afterthought, he walked over to the stove and enveloped her in a hug from behind. He looked both ways to see if they were perhaps being watched and, deciding that the coast was indeed clear, nuzzled her neck while whispering in her ear.

"Do you know how happy you've made me, *frau*?"

"Careful, you," she whispered her warning. "Maybe we should save the *shmuzzling* for the bedroom? She's getting older, ya know."

"Yes, I know that. Makes no difference, does it?" he asked.

"Yes, it does, you," she answered sternly, swatting his arm with a hot pad. He pouted, feigning dejection but quickly changed the subject.

"What's for breakfast? Do I smell *kaffi* soup?" Henry asked, running his fingers through his hairs.

"Yes, with biscuits, you like that," she said turning around and hugging him back.

Not one to miss this opportunity, he kissed her gently and could tell right away that she'd wanted to kiss him too. He kissed her in earnest until she pulled away, catching her breath.

"Enough now," she said. "It can wait. On another note, here Mister, she asked me to tell her about her *mamm* again. I think she is *chust* trying to understand where she fits into all of this," Veronica ventured.

"I know," Henry said nodding. "I think we just answer

what she asks, not much more till she's ready and asks again, sort of processing what she can handle at the time."

"I agree. I don't want it to be a big mystery either, but *chust* part of our story. And normal too. I think she can see how happy we are and how much she is loved and wanted. That's what every child needs. She isn't lacking there, I doubt," Veronica added.

"You're right, ya know. I've been thinking, too," Henry said as he took his seat at the head of the table. Veronica looked at him as she brought the bowls to the table, giving him leave to explain.

"There will always be things we need to figure out, but if we can keep the lines of communication open between you and me, we can tackle anything. I was so worried before we got married that I should have all the answers all the time. That was exhausting," he said, shaking his head.

"*Ach!* It sure was. I was ready to throw in the towel more than once for sure," Veronica remembered, shaking her head.

"I made it rather hard, I'm afraid, with all my specu-lating and pontificating. It could have been the end of us, ya know. But somehow you got the idea into your pretty head to *kumm* all the way to Canada and straighten me out, eh?" Henry added.

"I still don't believe I did that. Pretty gutsy if you ask me. It worked though, eh? With Aunt Wanda all agreeing with me," she remembered as she took two more mugs from the cupboard and set them on the table.

Just then Rose came skipping in, swinging the half-filled wire egg basket, still humming as the back door slammed shut with a thud. Her bare feet were covered with wet grass and her black *kapp* was already hanging down her back by its strings. Veronica stopped what she was doing to take in the toenails once again, incredulous at this child's imagination.

Not really all that different from how my own mind works, I guess, she thought to herself. *Wait till Henry hears about this one. Never a dull moment, eh?*

"The chicks haven't hatched yet but I left that one alone so she wouldn't peck me," Rose reported, holding out the wire basket for Veronica to take. Then she tipped her head and stood still in the middle of the kitchen frowning.

"I *chust* want to know how the eggs get there. I mean who puts them under the chickens for me to find?" she puzzled aloud. Henry and Veronica burst out laughing at that. Henry had to take his bandana handkerchief out of his pocket and wipe his eyes, still laughing.

"Sits ana," Veronica said, finally collecting herself, and called Rose to the table. "Hurry and wash first. It'll get cold."

When you flee temptation, don't leave a forwarding address.
~ Amish cookbook

CHAPTER 3

They've Arrived

"They're here!" Rose yelled up the stairs where Veronica had just laid down for a nap after a long morning fixing dinner, pre-soaking the wash, picking all the rhubarb from the garden and chopping it up besides—all five gallons of it.

"Mammmmm! Kumm!" she repeated from the bottom of the stairs by the kitchen while watching through the window as the huge semi maneuvered its way up to the barn.

This was special. This didn't happen everyday in their quiet, tranquil life. This was cause for excitement. Rose waited to see who would exit the cab and what would the contents of the truck be? She knew there were several orders in the works, her dat had mentioned it earlier in the week at supper, so she didn't know which one this could be.

Her *dat* heard it too and came running out of the paddock. Rose gave up trying to rouse Veronica, remembering her *dat* telling her earlier that day not to bother her *mamm,* that she needed her sleep, and opted to run out instead and watch Henry who was directing the truck to pull in backwards. Finally, it was in place and the driver put the engine in neutral, which kept the loud machine grinding away.

Hopping down from the cab he ran around to the back of the truck and opened the doors there. He pressed a button that activated a motorized lift that jutted out from under the doors. Jumping up on the lift he looked down at Henry who waved his hand to let him know it was in the right place. With that signal giving the go-ahead, the man started moving a small forklift that was inside the truck and would pick up each pallet and drive onto the lift with it. The lift would be lowered then, and the little forklift could be driven out with the pallet attached to the steel-pronged forks and delivered into the barn. The process was repeated for all the pallets until the last one sat inside the barn. The man gave Henry a clipboard to sign, ripped off a receipt and handed it to him. The canning jars had arrived. Enough for the coming canning season. Enough for every *frau* in the community.

Back in January Veronica had canvased the entire district, signing up everyone for their order and receiving their payments. Then she mailed in the order, adding an extra pallet because the numbers last year had been higher, and she was sure there would be requests around June or later asking if there were any left. The gardens often produced more than some bargained for, and you couldn't waste good food.

Henry came in as the mammoth truck left having deposited its load in the barn, but not before threatening to fall sideways as it waddled from side to side down the rained-out dirt driveway.

"Well, that's all done," he told Rose. "He confirmed the peaches and cherries from Michigan are still on time. Those will *kumm* late June or early August. Those will go into the cold barn where everyone can pick theirs up from there. We got plenty of ice blocks off the lake this past winter and the new insulation in there sure seems to be doing its job."

"I never get tired of canning," Veronica explained, smiling as she came out to join them by the barn.

"You sure it won't be too much for you this year? I don't want you overdoing it, ya know," he worried, switching to English.

"I'm not *sick*, Henry, only...well...you-know-what," she replied, glancing down at Rose. He nodded and smiled. This time he hadn't even winked, and she felt herself blushing.

A great deal of what we see depends on what we are looking for.
- Amish proverb

CHAPTER 4

Quilting Bee

Veronica had been looking forward to the quilting bee for weeks. Vernon and Holly would be married in a month's time. Holly's mother had begun cutting out squares since—what was it now?—must be years earlier. She had five daughters, so she figured she'd better start sooner than later and slowly get them going at least.

At breakfast that morning Veronica told Henry that they'd be going to the Masts right after breakfast. Rose gulped the grits with Red-eye Gravy that was in her mouth and announced that she was now old enough to babysit at the quilting bees so the moms could sew.

"Are you really?" Henry acted surprised. In fact, he really *was* surprised. Where had the time gone?

Red-eye gravy, one of Henry's all-time favorite breakfasts, is nothing more than fried county ham drippings and strong black coffee—yes, simmered together—which doesn't sound all that good if we only read about it. We learned to appreciate Red-eye gravy through tasting it, preferably drizzled onto a hot biscuit or bowl of hominy grits for breakfast.

"Well, the *mamms* are still there, but I get to play with 'my' baby the whole time when it isn't sleeping," she informed him. Then she frowned as she formulated her next question.

"Vernon and Holly are getting married, right?"

"That's right," Henry agreed, passing his bowl to Veronica for a refill.

"But do they have any *bobbeli* yet?" she wanted to know.

Henry was the first to answer. "No, of course not. They only *kumm* after they are married awhile," he explained.

"But how did *you* get married and already have *me?*" she wanted to know.

Henry stopped chewing his *mosch* and looked at Veronica for help on this one.

"Well," she began. "We've told you about your first *mamm,* right?"

"Ya. She died when I was *chust* a new *bobbel,*" Rose recited from memory. "But who took care of me then?" she asked.

Henry knew it was his turn to answer. "Well, your *grossmammi,* who's my *mamm,* came first and took care of you."

"And then she died," Rose said frowning and nodded her head.

"Ya, she did. And then we moved to Milo's and Edith was your *aendi,*" he said letting that sink in.

"So, I have four *mamms* or what? Becky, *Mammi,* Edith, and Veronica," she counted off on her fingers.

"Well," Veronica stepped in to rescue Henry at this point. "Becky was your first *mamm,* ya. And *Mammi* and Edith took such *gut* care of you, but *Mammi* was your *grossmammi* and Edith is your *aendi.*"

"And when you married me and *Dat,* then you are my real *mamm,* like?" she asked.

"Exactly," Veronica said. She figured that was about as

much as any four-year-old-almost-five-year-old could under-stand. Henry and Veronica knew this wouldn't be the end of the questions. Not by a long shot. They'd have their hands full with Rose and her questions into the next century.

Breakfast over, they all pitched in to tidy up the kitchen before Veronica and Rose would leave for their outing.

"I'll go *redd* up the horse," Henry said while wrestling his boots back on and headed for the barn. "Have fun, ladies," he called on his way out while plopping his straw hat on his head.

Finally on their way, the box with the Pork and Beans Cake they'd made the day before secured behind the front bench with a bungee cord.

"I bet no one's made that cake before. Do you think they'll like it?" Rose asked from the bench, sitting next to Veronica who held the reins with both hands.

"Well, Maudie only had it printed in *The Budget* earlier this week, so not many have had the time to try it out I'd wager," Veronica answered, "or even read it."

"But *Dat* sure liked it at breakfast, the little one you made for us." Then giggling, Rose said, "but you wouldn't tell him what was in it until after he tasted it, eh?"

"He still doesn't have a clue, does he?" Veronica chuck-led. She loved having a daughter she could conspire with. She knew she'd never take this one for granted.

"I set some out for him with his sandwiches for lunch. We can have him guess again when we see him at *zapper* tonight."

Rose nodded. "Whose baby will I get to watch do you think?" she asked as they clip-clopped along the road. Then she added, pouting, "The last time I babysat I got that fussy one, ya know. But it wasn't fun at all. I like fun *bobbeli,*" she continued pouting, her eyebrows frowning deep in thought. "Did I tell you he tried to *bite* me?"

"Well, he was *chust* teething. He couldn't help it," Veronica explained. That last statement brought up all the anguish of having lost her first baby all those years ago. *Close to nine years have passed now. How is that even possible?* Veronica asked herself as the horse continued on. *I would take a fussy* bobbel *any day over...* Veronica couldn't even say it, even after all these years. Her baby, Marta, had been born far too early with complications that ended her life when she was only three days old. Less than a decade ago they knew so little about prematurity, but since then are now able to treat hyaline membrane disease in newborn babies born before twenty-eight weeks successfully—and miraculously—often without any developmental delays like hearing impairment or mental challenges.

Finally, they arrived at the Mast's farm and parked along the wide drive. One of the big boys took the horse, watered him, and brought him into the field to join the others.

Rose offered to carry one of the twins that was handed to her from inside the buggy parked next to theirs.

"What's his name?" Rose asked.

"Oh, let's see," the frazzled mother swiped at the *schtruvvels* sticking to her forehead, and looked first at the baby in Rose's arms and then hoisting the second one out of the buggy said, "I think you've got Mary. I think this one's Martha. I try to keep a safety pin on Mary's *gaund...* I hope I didn't forget it in the rush of things at home. Oh, well. Soon enough they'll be able to tell me who they are, I guess," she stammered.

"But they could fool you then, too ya know, play tricks," Rose observed, chuckling.

"They wouldn't dare," their mother practically growled, frowning as she tucked the hairs back into her *kapp*. "At least let's hope not," she revised her statement, while shaking her distraught head.

"She's wrapped up tight like a burrito," Rose observed laughing.

"I think they like being all done up snug," their mother said balancing her bundle on her hip with one hand and reaching for the *kavli*.

Rose followed her then, clutching the precious little burrito in her arms.

Laden with the cake and a tray of cookies, Veronica led the way toward the house. Inside was quite the jolly gathering. Lots of offerings lined the counters and the long oak table in the kitchen while barefoot toddlers chased each other through the expansive rooms, shrieking with delight.

The quilt was stretched onto a standing frame and pinned in place with safety pins. Someone had spaced spools of quilting thread, scissors, dishes of thimbles and pin cushions with plenty of number eight quilting needles stuck into them, down the length of the center of the quilt within easy reach. Folding chairs and benches ringed the quilting frame.

It was a Bear Claws pattern quilt. The top had been pieced by the bride's mother over the past year. There were no curving lines in the pattern so it could be pieced on the treadle sewing machine. However, if you are making, for example, a Clamshell, a Dresden, or a Tumbling Blocks quilt, it is often easier to sew those by hand because of the sharp curves in the patterns. Though some Amish have devised ways to power a sewing machine using an air compressor, many still use the non-mechanized treadle machine they learned on growing up and feel perfectly comfortable using it.

"I'm thinking I should make them friendship bracelets with those tiny beads with letters on them with their names so their *mamm* can tie them on them and she won't get them mixed up," Rose said to Veronica when she brought her little one to show her. "She's got *ztzvilling!* Both girls, ya know. It's *ferhoodled.*"

"Oh, I'm sure their *mamm* knows them apart," Veronica said, slightly distracted by all the women coming into the house.

"Oh no, she doesn't. See, that is the thing," Rose explained.

"Well then, you could offer them to her," Veronica said, though she couldn't imagine a mother not knowing which twin is which, but then, maybe she really couldn't.

"Be sure to bring her to me before she fusses too much or she'll be too upset to feed," Mary (or perhaps Martha's) mother instructed Rose who was cradling one of them in her arms, though it seemed no one else there could tell them apart either.

"Absolutely no food from the tables, ya hear. He's allergic to nuts, but his *kavli* has his snacks and *esschtick* in there, too," another mother said as she handed the woven diaper basket to another girl holding her baby rather awkwardly who nodded back.

"Don't let him sleep more than two hours, please," another mother said to the girl standing next to Rose holding a husky little wood chopper who was flailing and trying his darndest to escape from her clutches.

"Don't let this one outta yer sight," yet another mother explained in no uncertain terms to another girl. "She's a runner. She'll go into the field to pet the stud bull if I'd let her."

Other instructions were being doled out until all the babysitters were released from the kitchen with their sweet little charges who now sounded more like little hellions by the minute, according to their mothers' declarations.

It was a beautiful sunny day. The girls tasked with babysitting gathered under the big red sugar maple tree in the yard, spreading blankets out on the grass while the *fraus* all celebrated their sudden freedom in the kitchen, oohing and aahing at all the delicious offerings there.

"Who made the raspberry cheesecake? That is my favorite. Bless you!" one mother said aloud to no one in particular.

"Is this corned beef pudding? Really?" called another mom.

After moving some of the pies over to make room, Veronica placed her cake on the table.

"And what did you make?" the *frau* next to her asked.

"It's called Pork and Beans Cake," she informed her.

"Are you kidding me? It sounds dreadful," the woman exclaimed rather loudly while frowning and scrunched her whole face.

"What did you call that?" another woman by the table turned toward Veronica and asked.

Several other women in the kitchen turned to see if they had heard correctly, too.

"It was in *The Budget* this week, Maudie's column," she

said almost apologetically. "She called it 'Pork and Beans Cake.'"

"Who'd wanna taste something called that? She could have named it something like, ya know, like...oh maybe, 'Surprise Cake,'" the first woman suggested.

"So, it really has pork and beans in it? Is it any *gut* though?" another mother asked while clutching her throat.

"My *halsband* wolfed it down this morning," Veronica vouched.

"But I bet you didn't tell him what was in it, did ya?" another woman chided.

"No, I made him guess and he couldn't, so I told him we'll continue tonight at *zapper* when we get home," Veronica explained, picking up a carrot cookie and taking a bite.

Slowly, as they all migrated to the quilting frame in the great room, the house became quiet while they took their seats around the masterpiece. Soon they were licking a finger to assist in threading the needles and began the monumental task in earnest. Coming to the quilt, finally Veronica looked at this tableau before her. The women were tall, short, dark-haired and blond or gray. All heads were bowed for the task ahead of them, as if in worship. The solid colors of the dresses created quite a display. There were no calicos or prints here. Greens, navy blue, gray, plum, royal blue, dusky rose, purple, Dutch blue, deep burgundy, black, and fawn brown all sat beside each other. Many wore glasses. All wore regulation starched white bonnets, though a couple were obviously sewn in a different style than the majority here but most likely those came from other communities, perhaps farther away. All had well-tanned arms and faces, evidence of spending hours in gardens and outdoor chores. Some were pleasantly plump, some quite thin, others clearly 'in the family way,' but should you ask when the momentous day might arrive, you will likely be told in no uncertain terms, "time will tell." Universally such intimate information is well guarded, thus ensuring that it won't become gossip among the women and go out into the wider community.

> *A Bible that is falling apart probably belongs to someone who isn't.*
> *- Amish saying*

CHAPTER 5

Robbing the Cradle

"Did you know that Sarabeth, that *maud* over at Eli and Hazel's is getting married too?" one woman named Ester asked those assembled at the quilt.

"No! Really? You mean that one that was such a worry when she first came here?" one grandmother asked.

"Do ya think we should make her a quilt too?" another woman questioned.

Veronica answered this one. "No, Faith told me Sarabeth's own *mamm* is doing it there, I guess in Ohio."

"Yes, her. They'd given up on her back in Ohio. They'd even tried that clinic, whatever it was called, 'Rest Home' something," Debra explained.

"I heard she came out to help Faith after that terrible train crash. I don't know how anyone could live with that. I don't know if I could..." Esther remarked as she frowned and squinted while attempting to thread her needle.

"But she was the *maud* and got along really well. I think she *chust* had to grow up, have some responsibility. Maybe her parents *chust* couldn't find their way with her. Anyway, the change of scenery for sure helped," another woman pondered aloud.

Hazel was at the quilt, too. "Well, Sarabeth is with us now. And I couldn't be happier with that *meedle*."

Veronica added, "she loves it there, ya know, Hazel. She's really a lovely girl. She'll always *chust* be herself. A bit unique, I guess."

"But a *hard* of gold," Hazel said, nodding. "We never had *kinner* but it's like we were waiting all this time *chust* for her. She and Benuel are a really *gut* match, too. They've even decided to get that lot down the road from us, the next farm over. He's working on the house there, totally converting it. Taking out the phone lines, the electricity, too. It's a cute house. She took me there a couple weeks ago. She'd never learned to sew—can you imagine?—but we've been plugging away it on my ancient Singer, and she's managed to sew the curtains now," Hazel said chuckling, the glowing pride in her protégé showing.

"The wedding is next month in Ohio. Eli and I are going, of course."

"Oh, Hazel, that's *wunderbar!*" Ester exclaimed. "But I heard that his *mamm* didn't give her blessing in the beginning. Not at all."

"That's what I heard too," Eunice added. "Not one little bit. His *mamm* knew Sarabeth's *mamm*—some distant cousin —and had the whole story on that girl. All they went through with her. Said it was positively hell. *Chust* about did the parents in, all those years. His *mamm* worried she wouldn't be faithful, being so flighty and all. And she'd been a terror once she hit her teens. What kind of *mamm* would she make? They even took her to all sorts of doctors, and no one knew what to do for her. His *mamm* tried her darnedest to get him to find another *frau*, but he wouldn't budge. She thought maybe the girl was bipolar, with her moods, or something inherited that she'd pass on to their *kinner.* Benuel *chust* stuck by his guns, he did. The girl had really gone after him and got what she wanted. His mother told me that Benuel didn't stand a chance once she got him in her clutches. Kind of sad, if you ask me. Some say, 'cradle snatching.' As if the boy didn't have any say in the matter at all."

Then another sister named Holly weighed in. "She really was an arrogant, pushy little thing, according to Millie at the Mercantile. Millie knows everything. The girl was impudent and presumptuous. A real flirt. No compass for appropriate social behavior. None at all. *Chust* marching to the tune of her own drum. I don't know where she got that from. Must have been something 'off' in that family."

Ester spoke up once more. "They say her parents were *chust* normal, that the other *kinner* turned out okay, I guess. Really *gut*. Something *chust* went wrong with Sarabeth."

"But Ester, that isn't true. Yes, Sarabeth is a strong-willed young woman, but that doesn't make her horrible," and then turning toward Hazel, Veronica asked, "I heard your Eli wasn't feeling too *gut*."

"He wasn't. It was *chust* dragging on and on but we got that nurse, Phoebe to *kumm* over and she took us to that nice nurse-practitioner lady who put him on all sorts of vitamins and something for the blood pressure and thyroid and he's as right as rain now. Much happier. Getting out more, too," she said.

"That is *gut* news," Debra remarked before continuing, "I was dead set against that girl going to college to be a nurse at the beginning, I was for sure, but I've really turned around on that one. Completely. It really is paying off, eh?"

"She came to ours when my Moses' mother was so ill,

and we had her at the house. Why, she helped us set up everything at home, moved *Mammi* downstairs and arranged all the help we'd need. Ordered a hospital bed, absolutely everything. It was only a month later that she died, but it's what she'd wanted, being at home."

"I couldn't have done it without Phoebe," another woman named Lillian said as she unwound more thread, snipped it and licked her finger to roll a knot at the end of it.

"Too bad she isn't a midwife, too. We could sure use one of those here," Heather's mother Nancy said.

"But Cashton isn't all that far away. And that clinic is growing. They have three birth rooms now. Have you seen it? It's quite fancy," Ester said. "They are even doing water births there. I can't imagine that. It's a wonder the babies don't drown!"

"But if you stop and think about it, babies have been in water for nine months. They don't take a breath until the cold air hits them in their face. So, when they are born into warm water, waiting for that cold air they still won't take a breath till they're lifted up out of it," Nancy said. "If you stop and think about it, it could work, ya know."

Then Debra weighed in. "I don't know. My doctor always just knocked me out when it got too painful. I was always happy with that."

"But those meds can affect the baby, don't ya know. Drugs them, too, making it harder for them to start up, ya know, breathe and all. I wouldn't touch the stuff with a ten-foot pole," Nancy said, quite horrified that so little was known about the drugs, and that many families trusted their doctors so unequivocally, as if they were all demigods that could do no wrong.

On barn raising: "We give each other our labor. We look forward to raisings. There are so many helping, no one has to work too hard. And we get in a good visit."
~ Gene Logsdon, Whole Earth Review, Spring 1986

CHAPTER 6
Pork and Beans Cake &
Wedding Salsa

I t was already noon.

"My, but time flies, eh?" Naomi said as she scooped up a generous serving of each of the dessert offerings spread out on the kitchen table, until she could not find any more space for more on her plate. The toddlers were being given lunch outdoors on the blankets under the big maple. Their babysitters were eating lunch too, between shoveling mouthfuls into their little charges. The tiny babies were upstairs in one of the bedrooms being nursed while their *mamms* balanced their plates on their knees, and cake crumbs were falling on their downy heads.

It had been a productive morning. They would still sew another hour or so before packing up and heading home to make supper. The noon meal back at each farm had all been made ahead and arranged under cotton dish towels (to keep the flies off) for the men there. Fresh bread, cold cuts, cheeses, purple eggs and beets, potato salad, coleslaw and a generous dessert were waiting for the men at home when they knocked off work at dinnertime.

"Who made the German noodle casserole?" one woman

asked. "Are these poppy seeds in it? My favorite." Ruth hesitantly held up her hand. "Hope you like it," she said rather sheepishly.

Another woman said to no one in particular, "Oh. Is it? It is! Glorified Rice. What a treat!" And so the line of *fraus* progressed through the buffet offerings.

"Who made the Wedding Salsa? They did a super job on it," Susanna complimented it while looking around to see if anyone would own up to it.

"Really, whose is it?" Then Ruby waved her hand above her head. "I *chust* make mine with tomatoes, bell peppers, onions, cider vinegar, jalapeno peppers—depending on how hot you like it, sugar—or honey, kosher salt, fresh garlic, fresh oregano, and pepper. I make it in an iron pot. You can also add corn, black beans or crushed pineapple for a different flavor altogether," she explained while Susanna nodded and took that in.

Seated on chairs, sofas and benches away from the quilt they enjoyed their lunch. The times they were together like this were so few and far between. Sometimes they'd be home for weeks at a time, especially in winter, venturing out only to every other Sunday church. This was for certain a treat and they would savor every single minute, for sure.

One woman walked around the room topping off everyone's coffee while some went back for seconds. Then, one by one they'd drift toward the desserts lined up by the dry sink. They were all conscious of the fact that they shouldn't indulge, especially as many were in the process of attempting to lose some of their 'baby fat' after the last pregnancy, but this was just too good to pass up. They'd go back on their diets tomorrow, they told themselves. Tomorrow. Promise.

"You brought this cake, didn't you Veronica?" one

woman asked holding up her fork with the moist dark cake with cream cheese icing on it.

"Yes. Do you like it?" Veronica asked. She knew what was coming.

"It's *wunderbar-gut!*" the woman replied.

"It really is," said another woman name Bertha. "What's all in it?"

"A can of Pork and Beans," Veronica answered and held her breath. At that the whole room became quiet. Several forks clinked as they were quickly returned to their plates.

"No. You're joshing me," Bertha said.

"Where did you even get that idea, anyway?" a young mother named Rachel asked.

"Okay, Veronica. Spill the beans. Tell us!" demanded a grandmother named Grettel.

Every head was now turned toward Veronica.

"Maudie's column in *The Budget* this week," Veronica said, almost apologetically.

Before she could answer another woman said, "Oh, I saw that. It sounded positively vile, though. But this is *gut,*" she said, genuinely surprised. "Did the column say who sent it in to Maudie or where they were from?"

"Ya, let me think. I believe it was someone called Faith from West Virginia."

"So, how does that work?" Bertha asked.

"Well," Veronica began. "You drain a fifteen ounce can of pork and beans, ya know, the juice and pick out the fat bits. Then you mash or blend it with an eight ounce can of crushed pineapple—*with* the pineapple juice—and add sugar, four eggs, oil, baking soda, cinnamon, flour, baking powder and I added a little salt," Veronica explained.

"It tastes kinda like a carrot cake...well, sort of," Bertha said.

"Or maybe like a spice cake, ya think?" the grandmother

asked while pushing her glasses further up on her nose and examining the cake on her fork once more. Then adding to no one in particular she said, "why, I never...."

"Did you see about that accident in *The Budget?*" Naomi asked. "Ben Schwartz over in Clarion was thrown off a manure spreader when the neck yoke snap unhooked, and the horses ran away. They worried about his heart, so he went to the ER. He was badly bruised but nothing broken. Not sure how he landed, though. He was lucky, for sure, I guess."

Heads nodded around the room. Then the plates and mugs were collected and stacked by the sink. They could wait till later. There was a quilt to finish first.

Seated at the quilt once more they continued their various conversations, trying to eke out the last moments of this special time together.

Then it was time for the women and their children to head home. Diapers were changed, and the older ones, not quite ready for school yet, were ordered to make one last trip to the outhouse. Food was packed up and little arms stuffed into sweaters and jackets. Hats were tied under unwilling little chins, evidenced by the general outcry heard by all. Veronica made one last sweep of the house, gathering any truant toys or sneakers. She found a few lost possessions and one abandoned *kavli*. There was a miniature plastic pig, a well-worn faceless doll, a pacifier, and a small navy sneaker that had lost its sole mate. She ran out to the buggies and returned the items to their respective owners.

It had been a good day. Good friends, good food and fellowship.

It's a little too little to save,
And a little too much to dump,
There's nothing to do but eat it,
And that makes the housewife plump.
- from an Amish cookbook.

CHAPTER 7
Friend or Foe?

Halfway through supper that night, Rose asked Henry something else she had been puzzling about.

"*Dat,* tell me again why you said the potatoes and the tomatoes can't be planted next to each other. It's not like they're enemies or animals or anything, is it?"

"No, they're not," Henry patiently explained, "but Nature somehow has arranged it so that the plants help each other out. We plant zinnias because they attract ladybugs who can easily wipe out all the aphids and cabbage flies that want to eat our vegetables. In the same way parsley protects asparagus from beetles. And marigolds scare away the bugs that attack the roots of tomato plants and other vegetables. But radishes don't do so well next to cabbage. Don't ask me why. And dill and basil protect tomato plants from the tomato horn worm. Oh, and mint repels ants and cabbage moths. I'll get the article after we eat."

"What is this I'm eating, anyway?" Henry asked after his next bite.

"I made it with *Mamm*," Rose informed him. "It's called Ramen Salad. Do you like it?"

"I do. But I don't know what it is. Gummy worms or something?" he asked, holding a forkful up from his plate.

"No, silly," Rose replied. "It's those Japanese noodles. Ramen. Do you like it?" she insisted.

"Well, let me see," he teased and popped a forkful into his mouth. "Mmmm, hmmmm," was all he could answer, nodding vigorously.

"I think he means he does, *Mamm*," Rose concluded, giggling. "And I made the soup. *Mamm* said she'll teach me how to make White Christmas Pie, too. But not now. Not until closer to Christmas."

"So, what's in the soup?" Henry prodded Rose.

Gulping what she had in her mouth, she explained. "Well, it's cheese soup with broccoli. The popcorn goes on top. Isn't it yummy?" she asked. Henry nodded his head, his eyebrows raised, with googly eyes teasing her, as he slurped another spoonful.

"Here it is," Henry shook out the newspaper when he found the article he was looking for. "It's from last week's *Budget*. A *frau* writes such interesting tidbits in a column there each week. It's called, 'Just Mom.'" Then he began to read.

"She says here she found it in a greenhouse in Michigan where she lives.

Peas don't like a lot of water.
Potatoes and tomatoes are not friends—at all.

Potatoes don't like cucumbers either. Not sure if they like anyone.

Cabbage and potatoes are friends. Okay, so they aren't totally unsociable.

Beans should not be planted with onions, or beets for that matter.

However, carrots love beans as a neighbor.

Beets and onions are friends.

Beets and cabbage are buddies.

Beets and potatoes get along swell.

Tomatoes love carrots.

Tomatoes adore peas.

Carrots and onions are fast friends.

Radishes do not wish to be near cabbage. Snobs!

Marigolds make a great border to help repel pests for all plants.

Here are also some of the companion plants for vegetables in your garden. Some, like zinnias, are plants we have used for years.

Dill and Basil are natural protectors of tomato plants and repel that awful creature known as the tomato horn worm. Yuck!

Mint repels both ants and cabbage moths.

Zinnias attract ladybugs which are a very beneficial insect who can easily eradicate aphids and cabbage flies among other bugs.

Marigolds are a great companion to any vegetable, especially tomatoes as it repels ne...ma...todes that often attack the roots of the plant."

Henry stopped to think about that. "I don't have a clue what those are, much less pronounce it. Anyway, we can look it up in the dictionary after." Then he continued.

"'Nasturtiums will attract aphids, keeping them away from nearby vegetables.

Basil, when planted about a foot from tomatoes, has been shown to increase the yield of tomatoes and when planted near lettuce will improve the flavor.

Parsley protects asparagus from beetles.

Rosemary deters bean beetles.

Chives planted near carrots improve their flavor.

Chamomile improves the growth and flavor of onions.

Horseradish planted near potatoes increases disease resistance.

Bee Balm improves the growth and flavor of tomatoes.

And last, but not least, she writes here: 'Composted beet leaves add significant magnesium to the soil when mixed in. Magnesium is important to the photosynthesis process.'

Whew! How do you keep track of all that when you're planting a garden?" Henry asked.

"Easy," Veronica said. "You make a chart ahead of time and be sure and date it each year you make it. I can imagine you can rotate your crop each year by moving the rows around but keep them next to their so-called 'friends.' I can start the chart in the winter when we order the seeds. The catalogues should be arriving any day now for next year."

"Along with every Amish *frau* who reads *The Budget* across North America," Henry added, sarcastically.

"It sounds like *fun*. I'll find my graph paper in the morning," she said.

"Fun? Really?" Henry questioned, incredulously.

"You know how I relish a challenge," Veronica replied.

And then that little voice once more: "Can I help too?"

"*May* I help," Veronica corrected, ever the teacher.

"*Dat?*" Rose asked, giving up on getting a definitive answer from her mother.

"So, what can we do next, *Mamm?*" Rose asked as she dried the dishes while standing on her little stool at the sink.

"For one thing, you are having a bath, Missy," Veronica told her. Rose reached over and swiped at the soap bubbles with one finger and quickly daubed some of the little bubbles onto Veronica's nose, catching her completely unawares, as she said, "there! Put a pat of butter on your nose!"

"What does that mean?" Veronica asked when she managed to stop laughing and wiped her nose off with the back of her hand.

"Oh, nothing," Rose answered, chuckling. Then she continued.

"But I mean for Christmas, is what I wanted to know. What comes next?" Rose repeated her question.

"Well, I *chust* remembered another story I read to my students when I was teaching. I think I can find it in the closet. It's about something I am hoping to do next for Christmas," Veronica said. "I *chust* don't know if we'll manage it this year, though."

"Can you tell me? Or is it a secret?" Rose wanted to know.

"It's a secret. But I'll find it tomorrow, if I kept my copy, that is," Veronica assured her.

"May I hear it too?" Henry asked, intrigued by this mysterious story. "I am always up for a *gut* story."

A mother is a gardener of God tending to the hearts of her children.
- Amish proverb

41

CHAPTER 8
Potato Prints

Veronica finished cleaning the kitchen after dinner and stood surveying the room as she dried her hands on a towel. *Well, that's done,* she told herself, deciding there was nothing else to do there.

She heard little feet bounding down the creaky stairs. Sure enough, Rose skipped into the kitchen, her work apron still tied on.

"Ready?" she asked. "This'll be so much fun!" Rose declared.

"Okay, you go get the brown grocery bags on the shelf in the mud room, and I'll set the irons," Veronica said.

She set two sadirons on the stovetop of the cookstove and checked the fire box there, adding a small log. Next, she opened the ironing board that she'd brought to the kitchen from her sewing room within reach of the stove.

"Now you go to the root cellar and bring up the two biggest potatoes you can find there."

"Okay," Rose answered, happily skipping over to the basement steps.

While she was gone, Veronica spread out each brown

bag, cutting the bottom off first. Then she slit them up the side, opening the whole sheet of brown paper. Thus, they were ready to iron. She picked up a sadiron and proceeded to iron the wrinkles out of the first one. Returning the now-cooled-off sadiron to the stovetop she picked up the other iron and proceeded to the next brown bag. Soon she had all of them ready for the next step as Rose came back upstairs, a potato in each hand.

"What took you so long?" Veronica wanted to know.

"I was counting the jars. We still have five pickles and only six applesauce. And only a couple of Traffic Jams. Did you know?" she asked.

"Yes, *daumling*. We'll be canning for another year before you know it," Veronica said.

"Oh, I can't wait!" Rose hopped up and down, clapping her hands.

"Let's *chust* hope you're still that excited to do the canning ten years from now," Veronica said cynically, remembering all her peevishness when she was a teenager and had to help with the unending bushels of vegetables and fruits, often on the hottest days of summer. The kitchen would feel like an oven with kettle after kettle of water boiling to seal the jars, usually only seven jars at a time, over and over, repeatedly, until every flat surface and table in the room was covered with towels and rows and rows of jars lined up there waiting to cool down.

Back to the task at hand, it was time to carve the potatoes. Cutting them in half the short way, versus the length or long way, Veronica demonstrated the process for Rose. Then it was Rose's job to dry off each raw white surface with a towel.

"What designs do you think?" Veronica asked.

"Oh, snowmen and a bell and a girl gingerbread cookie

and a mitten? Or maybe a *Grischtdaag* tree, or a stocking?" Rose suggested.

"Well, perhaps we should skip the tree. We don't have *Grischtdaag* trees here, so maybe don't suggest it on a card," Veronica hesitantly countered Rose's suggestion of a tree.

"Okay. But that's five," Rose pointed out, "And we only have four potato stamps to do it all...but I see *Grischtdaag* trees when we go to town shopping. Why don't we have trees? They are so pretty. How come we don't, *Mamm?* Why?"

"Well, yeah. Why don't we have Christmas trees? *Gut* question, *liebling*. First off, what do they say about a Baby born in a manger who came to save us all?" Veronica struck out into the very controversial topic. Some Amish, wanting to modernize, actually do have trees, though without electricity the lights are a no-brainer. They are decorated with homemade ornaments. Carved wooden animals, cut out stars with glitter glued to each side, strings of popcorn and cranberries, paper chains, gingerbread cookies strung up with ribbon. Other families have even welcomed Santa and his reindeer, leaving snacks out for both. But many feel it is not the direction that the Amish should go.

Veronica remembered just then visiting a store one Christmas that had a small tree. The store was run by an immigrant family. *Were they from Southeast Asia somewhere? Laos or Cambodia?* She tried to remember but couldn't, though she did remember they had decorated the tree with things from the shop, the baby pacifiers being the most absurd things on the tree, she remembered, chuckling. At least they were easy to hang on a tree with the large hole in the handle part.

On the other hand, more conservative Amish continued to celebrate while emulating their orthodox predecessors, with greenery and ribbons, candles and cookies and candy.

And of course, reading the Nativity story from the Bible. Families visited one another and feasted and ate some more and visited some more. *Youngie* went caroling, singing their little hearts out and held skating parties with bon fires until all hours of the morning. No one cared if they had to be up for the morning milking at four a.m. This was Christmas!

Second Christmas came on January sixth, the day reserved for the three kings' arrival to worship the Baby and bring Him gifts. This was when the homemade and not-so-homemade gifts came out of their hiding places to delight all. Again, there was singing and feasting and visiting with the addition of gifts this time, some having been secretly made as far back as the summer.

Just before school let out for the holidays, the children would be kept very busy memorizing their parts for the school play, painting props for it, composing programs and creating costumes. Mothers would be relegated to the costume brigade and tasked also to contribute snacks for after the play. All the students' families came on the appointed night. The little scholars had waited for this for a very long time. It was the highlight of the year.

"So, next year when you start school, you'll even get to be in the Christmas play. *Chust* think, Rose." Veronica felt the tears gathering once more. She loved Rose with all her heart. Then it occurred to her. Would she love this new baby as much too? Would Rose? Or would she be jealous of him or her? Resentful of the baby taking away her doting mother and her coveted position as the only child?

"So, then, we *chust* might have to get another potato," Veronica said. Rose instantly popped up from her chair at the mention of potatoes, ready to fly down the stairs to the root cellar.

"Let's *chust* do these first. We can always add one later, eh?" Veronica said, reining in Rose back to the table.

Always the little optimist, Rose readily agreed, nodding her head.

"Now we must carve out from *around* the picture. I'll draw the bell with a marker first. Then we have to carefully cut away whatever we *don't* want in the picture, the background. That will leave only the bell which we can then paint over and print on the paper." Rose nodded as she watched, though she hadn't quite grasped how it all worked yet. Veronica would show her.

"I used to do this with my students when I was a teacher," Veronica informed Rose. "When we're done with the potato prints, we'll make some with cookie cutters dipped in the same Tempera paint. Then we can do horses and stars and all sorts. When they're done on the brown bag paper they almost look like gingerbread cookies," she explained.

"But we can't eat them," Rose added chuckling.

"Nope. You better not. You'll get a tummy ache then," Veronica pointed out.

"And you promised to teach me how to make snowflake coffee filters, remember?" Rose said.

"Oh, I almost forgot those!" Veronica said, feigning ignorance.

"Because we can put those in the windows and tape up all the cards we get around the doors," Rose remembered being told all the things they would do to prepare for Christmas. Veronica got out the old chopping block paper cutter from her school days.

"We have to make them into cards before we print on them," Veronica explained.

"See," Veronica demonstrated. "About nine inches by six after we fold them. It has to fit into the envelopes we bought."

"I've drawn some of the lines on this brown paper. Then we bring it over to the paper cutter and cut on the lines, but no fair cutting off your finger, okay? Then you fold them in half long wise. We'll do the first few together."

Rose nodded again as Veronica explained the whole process.

"Okay. Here is your first stamp. See the bell is standing up on the potato and the space around the bell is all cut away." Rose nodded again. "Now you *chust* dip the bell in the paint here on this plate and then print it on the paper like this," Veronica demonstrated.

"Okay," Rose readily agreed as she bit her tongue and carefully, slowly made the first card. Completely pleased with herself she then laid the potato down on the table and skipped around the kitchen.

"Can we make *Grischtdaag* cookies now? And then snowflakes, and then *Dat's* presents, too?" she asked.

"Whoa there. I think all we can manage *chust* now is one project a day. We still have a few weeks for all of that, probably two months. Let's do as many cards as we can today and then decide what's next. Ya know, we still have to do all the normal stuff, you know, like clean the house, and do the laundry and make dinner and...."

Rose cut in, "and pick the last kale and find mushrooms too!"

"Exactly. One *Grischtdaag* project a day is plenty. You'll see," Veronica said. As they printed the Christmas cards, they were carefully spaced out on the table so they could dry.

"Won't *Dat* be surprised?" Rose asked, unable to stand still but jumped up and down instead.

"I suppose he will be that." Veronica smiled. She gazed at Rose then. Her very own daughter. For all time. *He does wipe every tear away. Denki, Gott,* she sent up a quick prayer. *Denki.*

Our duty is not to see through one another but to see one another through.
- Amish saying

CHAPTER 9
A Christmas Memory

Veronica did actually find the book she was looking for. After supper the next night they all settled in *die gut shtup*. It was raining. Storming quite seriously, you could say. Thunder and lightning and wind to beat the band. There hadn't been a storm like this in recent years.

"*Dat,* is it raining cats and dogs?" Rose wanted to know. At that Henry got up and walked to the window to look out, feigning surprise.

"Well, I don't see any. *Chust* trees bent over and a bit of hail. It's a gut one, I'd say," he said.

"Maybe we could adopt a couple if any *kumm* along," Veronica wondered aloud.

"What could we adopt?" Rose wanted to know.

"Cats or dogs, I think she means," her *dat* clarified, chuckling.

"Do I get to name them all?" Rose asked expectantly.

"Of course," her *dat* agreed, shaking his head.

Henry looked over Rose's head where she sat between them. He caught Veronica's eye then and winked. She blushed. Even after all these months, those feelings hadn't died down. Not at all. Truth be told, they could both say they were even more in love than ever. Love only grew in this house. *How did I get so lucky, anyway?* Veronica thought to herself as she gazed into his twinkling eyes. *It's not really luck,* she told herself. *But then, that'd be heresy. It's all* Gott, *not luck. His gifts over and over. Giving me a family again after losing so much. Healing my heart, and Henry's heart, too.* She felt the tears welling up—would they never stop? *Good time to excuse myself,* she told herself getting up from the couch. Scurrying barefoot to the kitchen she poured three mugs of cocoa from the pan that had been sitting on the cookstove and carried those on a tray along with the bowl of popcorn she'd made earlier. They would make a night of it.

"*A Christmas Memory,* by Truman Capote," Veronica began. "Imagine a morning in late November. A coming of winter morning more than twenty years ago. Consider the kitchen of a spreading old house in a country town. A great black stove is its main feature, but there is also a big round table and a fireplace with two rocking chairs placed in front of it. Just today the fireplace commenced its seasonal roar.

"A woman is standing at the kitchen window. She is small and sprightly, like a bantam hen, but, due to a long youthful illness, her shoulders are pitifully hunched. Her face is remarkable—not unlike Lincoln's, craggy like that, and tinted by sun and wind; but it is delicate too, finely boned, and her eyes are sherry-colored and timid. "Oh my," she exclaims, her breath smoking the windowpane, 'it's fruitcake weather!'"

"What's 'fruitcake weather'?" Rose wanted to know.

Veronica explained. "In the story they tell you about how they get ready for Christmas each year and their tradition of making fruit cakes."

"*Chust* them? Not the family?" Rose asked.

"No. Their family isn't very nice. It is *chust* the two of them getting ready," Veronica said. She continued reading.

"The person to whom she is speaking is myself. I am seven; she is sixty-something, we are cousins, very distant ones, and we have lived together—well, as long as I can remember. Other people inhabit the house, relatives, and though they have power over us, and frequently make us cry but we are not, on the whole, too much aware of them. We are each other's best friend. She calls me Buddy, in memory of a boy who was formerly her best friend. The other Buddy died in the 1880's, when she was still a child. She is still a child."

"Why is she still a child?" Rose was puzzled.

"Because she is such a sweet lady, I guess. Maybe a bit simple," her *dat* said.

"That's *baremlich*," Rose countered.

"Let me *chust* read," Veronica requested.

The story continued. "I knew it before I got out of bed," she says, turning away from the window with purposeful excitement in her eyes.

"The courthouse bell sounded so cold and clear. And there were no birds singing; they've gone to warmer country, yes indeed. Oh, Buddy, stop stuffing cookies and fetch our buggy. Help me find my hat. We've thirty cakes to bake."

So, the story goes. Veronica stops reading to interject a further explanation after taking a sip of cocoa.

"Their buggy isn't actually a horse and buggy. It's a baby buggy. An old creaky pram," she says.

"What's that for, then?" Rose asks.

"You'll see," she says as she continues explaining.

"In the story they go off into the woods and find nuts and hike to the store for the rest of the ingredients after counting all their pennies they've been saving that they hide in a purse under the old lady's bed, under the floorboard, that's under the chamber pot. They also collect some of the harder to find things from a neighbor and start making the fruit cakes. It takes them days to make. When they are finally finished, they consult their list of people they've sent fruit cakes to over the years. Some are very famous people who write back thanking them for the cakes."

That year Veronica and Rose managed to make a dozen fruit cakes, too. They delivered one to their friendly doctor in town and one to Eli and Hazel. Another one barely fit into the mailbox, its label reading, "For our mailman friend. Merry Christmas!" They also mailed some to other people. Hilary Clinton wrote back as did Mr. Rogers whose books they liked to check out at the library. The Cat in the Hat *and* Dr. Seuss also wrote back thank you notes that year. Thus, a tradition was born in Veronica's family.*

* *This tradition also extends to the author's family who received thank you letters from the above-named people over the years, among others.*

CHAPTER 10
Whoopie Pies

"I never sawd them before," Rose said as she knelt on the fresh hay on the *hinklehaus* floor and gazed into the chicken box.

"If we're quiet, she'll let us watch," Veronica said.

Rose switched to a whisper. "Ya sure they're gonna *kumm* out today? How'd you know?"

"First, if you listen very carefully, you'll hear the tiny pecking sounds," she explained.

"Then you look when the hen stands up. You'll see cracks or holes they've made with their tiny beaks on the larger end of the egg."

"Then what?" Rose whispered.

"Then each chick pecks and pecks around the whole end until it's almost a perfect circle."

"They all know how to do it? Do they hear their *mamm* through the shell? Or do they *chust* know?" Rose wondered.

"*Gott* tells every creature how to do it. How to get born. It's pretty amazing, eh?" Veronica asked. Rose nodded her head. It was more than amazing. It was a miracle.

"Then what happens?" Rose wanted to know.

"Well, when they are close to being done pecking in a circle, their little feet and wings help push them out and the shell 'lid,' what is still attached, acts as a door and your chick pops through," Veronica explained.

"Wow. I hear more pecking. Do you?" Rose asked.

"Yup. I do. See the hen does too. She's standing up to look at all the commotion underneath her. See, you can see the little holes and cracks getting bigger," Veronica pointed out.

"Oh! Look! That one's *kumming* out. *Mamm,* look!" Rose squeaked.

"HE'S OUT!" she shrieked.

"Shhh!" Veronica hushed her.

"Then, how do you know the girls from the boys?" Rose wanted to know, asking without taking her eyes off the emerging chicks.

"We'll know better when they grow up a bit," Veronica said.

"I remember watching the cat have babies. She had only three. This hen will have, let me see," she said, silently counting on her fingers.

"Ten! Ten whole chicks!" Then Rose frowned, obviously deep in thought.

"*Mamm,* was I borned in the shell or outta the shell?"

Veronica laughed then. Rose was distracted by two more chicks falling out of their shells and wobbling their over-sized heads on their tiny skinny necks, like bobble head figures on the shelves at the pharmacy in town, while awkwardly stretching out tiny wet wings.

"Can I hold one?" Rose asked.

"Maybe tomorrow. Look, we should go in now. We can check back later, maybe after supper, ya? We'll give the hen some time alone with her chicks," Veronica explained.

"They *chust* look like iddy bitty birds. Where are their feathers?" Rose asked.

"They will grow up a little every day. You'll see," she promised.

"Okay. But *Mamm,* who gets to name them all?"

"I guess you will, eh?" Veronica helped Rose up and they quietly went back to the house carrying the other eggs they had collected earlier.

"So, what are we doing for *Grischtdaag* today?" Rose asked as soon as they were back in the kitchen.

"Well, tell you what. Let's make Whoopie pies first and then we can decide on *Grischtdaag?* Okay?" Veronica asked.

Rose whined, "Why do we have to make Whoopie pies anyway? I wanna get ready for *Grischtdaag,*" she moaned.

"Because we are having some special guests for the weekend," Veronica told her.

"Who? Who's *kumming?*" Rose perked up but then looked at Veronica sideways, wary of this new development.

"You'll see. But we can't tell *Dat*. It's a surprise for him, too."

"Why can't you tell me?" Rose challenged.

"Because I don't want it accidentally slipping out and have him find out, that's why," Veronica said. "Listen, I will tell you tomorrow after dinner when he goes back to the barn. As soon as he leaves. I promise. I am hoping they'll be here in time for *zapper* later in the afternoon."

"Oh, alright. Do I know them?" Rose asked.

"Uh-huh," Veronica answered. "But I really need your help making a mess of pies. Go get your apron, okay?"

"But why are they called Whoopie pies anyway?" Rose

grumped, dragging her bare feet toward the row of hooks behind the stove where the aprons lived.

"Well, I guess a long time ago, a little boy or a little girl opened their lunch pail and found one in their lunch and threw it up in the air and yelled, 'Whoopie.' I'm told that's how they got the name," Veronica explained as she took out bowls and rolling pins and various ingredients. "We'll wrap each one up in Saran and they'll keep *chust* fine that way."

"I like the chocolate kind," Rose informed Veronica handing her the ties from her apron to secure in the back.

"I guess that's what we'll make. I'm low on oats and pumpkin so I can't make those kinds today, anyway," Veronica explained as she tied on the apron and then continued assembling everything they would need to make the giant marshmallow fluff-filled cookies.

Then as an afterthought, Veronica suggested they make coffee filter snowflakes to tape in the windows while the cookies are baking and then cooling. With company coming it would make the house rather festive, though it wasn't even snowing outside yet.

"Goodie, that will be fun," Rose said, now slightly more agreeable.

A smile is such a powerful weapon, you can even break ice with it.
- Amish saying

CHAPTER 11
Yummasetti

"Okay, now," Rose put her fork down with an attitude and faced Veronica.

"Now you *must* tell me who's *kumming*. You promised," Rose reminded her. "*Dat's* gone to the barn and dinner is over, remember?"

"There's no reason to get huffy, Missy," Veronica told her in no uncertain terms. *This one isn't even five yet...with an attitude...what will it be like when she's fifteen? Lord help us!* Veronica thought to herself.

"Well, your cousins, for one. And their new *bobbel*," Veronica answered, smiling.

Rose jumped up from her seat, clapping and then bouncing around the kitchen like a spring lamb.

"Really? They're really *kumming* here? Will they remember me?" Rose said. Without waiting for a reply, she continued as she spun and danced around the kitchen.

"I haven't seen them in a coon's age, *Mamm*. That's why we had to clean the house all week and make Whoopie pies, eh? And wash all the sheets...and...and I even had to sweep the outhouse. Oh, I'm so excited!" she said, unable to contain her absolute glee.

"When will they be here, ya think?"

"Sometime before supper, I reckon. Now help me with these dishes and we'll make a start on supper," Veronica said getting up from the table.

"Today? Really? They're *kumming* today? I don't believe it!" she squealed.

"What are we gonna make? You put those hard-boiled eggs in the beet pickle yesterday. And you made rolls yesterday too. Will we make another Pork and Beans cake too?" Rose rambled on.

"First things first," Veronica said. "Help me bring the dishes to the sink, please."

"Then we'll start on supper," she gently continued, hoping in vain to bring the excitement level down a few notches.

"We should have Yummasetti, *Mamm*. Do you think they'll like that?" Rose asked.

"Everyone likes that. Yes, let's make that," Veronica agreed, surprising herself. *A cook already. When did she grow up?* she thought to herself.

"And pickles and rolls and dessert. What should we make for dessert?" the little chef inquired.

"Let's *chust* start the main dish first," Veronica said. "Dishes," she said a bit more firmly this time. Rose carefully stacked the dirty plates on the table and carted those to her *mamm* standing at the sink. Then she grabbed all the used utensils and serving spoons and shuttled those to the sink too. The last thing was the cups. After bringing those to be washed she caught a soapy dish rag that Veronica volleyed to her across the kitchen where the child deftly caught it midair. After scrubbing off the oil cloth tablecloth, she threw the dish cloth back across the kitchen toward Veronica where it landed squarely on one of her shoulders.

"*Gut* pitch there. You get to be on the baseball team when you start school," Veronica said.

Then Rose dragged her wooden step stool across the linoleum kitchen floor to the sink and climbed up on it to begin swishing the dishes through the rinse water and then dried it all.

"We could put out the Traffic Jam for the rolls. I love all those berries mixed up in it. Do you think they'll like that?" she queried.

"Ya. Thanks, we'll get that up," Veronica agreed. Then, just at the mention of it Rose jumped off the step stool and skipped to the root cellar door and was gone in an instant, returning only seconds later with the jam.

"*Denki, daumling,*" Veronica said as Rose again took up her place at the sink.

Then, the back door opened, and Henry stood there.

Veronica quickly whispered in Rose's ear, "Don't say a peep, okay?" Rose nodded.

"So, what are you two up to?" Henry asked.

"*Chust* dishes," Veronica answered. Rose agreed without looking at him, "*Chust* dishes."

"You're back..." Veronica inquired, praying Rose could keep their surprise under wraps just a little longer.

"Got any leftover *kaffi*? I could use some," Henry explained.

"Sure. Let me reheat it for you," Veronica offered, placing a small saucepan on the stove and pouring in the coffee from the thermos still at the table. "It'll be cold by now," she commented. It was ready in minutes.

"So what's up this afternoon? You ladies have any plans?" Henry asked, taking the mug from Veronica and pouring milk in from the pitcher still sitting on the table.

She was quick to answer before Rose who could possibly, inadvertently divulge their secret.

"Oh, ya know, the regular and all," she hedged. Rose agreed, "ya, you know."

"Okay. See you gals for *zapper* then," he said. Noticing Rose intent on rinsing the dishes, he winked at Veronica. She winked back and immediately found herself blushing.

"Not now." she scolded him.

"*Pennsylfaani* please," Rose said without looking up, not having understood the part of their exchange spoken in English which she was still learning.

Henry stifled a laugh behind his mug as he took a sip of the hot coffee while Veronica said firmly addressing Rose, "Not everything here is said for little ears, you know."

Then Henry asked Rose who was climbing off the step stool, "Say, why don't you go check on your chicks? Let me know how many she has now. Here, wait. Take the egg basket and check on the others. I heard quite a racket when I came by *chust* now. Ya know how they announce that they're laying? Some like to lay in the morning and some later in the day."

Rose didn't need another word. She ran across the kitchen and was out the door in seconds, letting the screen door slam once again, but not before her black *kapp* flew off her head and landed on the mud room floor. When she was gone Henry asked, "How are ya feeling today?"

"Oh, blah. Ya know, but it usually goes away by noonish. It'll get better."

Vee get too soon oldt, undt too late schmart.
- Amish proverb

CHAPTER 12

Gummy Worms

The Yummasetti in the oven and the table set, Veronica surveyed the kitchen, hoping she hadn't forgotten some vital item there. It was starting to cool off outside with the sun hovering over the horizon. Rose had been sitting in the great room window seat anxiously waiting for their guests. Rosemary was propped up next to her facing the window, also.

"What if they're late?" she asked loud enough for Veronica to hear in the kitchen.

"Well, they called and left a voicemail at the phone shack this morning saying they were still planning to be on time. I guess we *chust* must trust that then," Veronica replied.

"How old is their *bobbel* now?" Rose asked.

"She'd be probably about, let me see, around two or three months now," Veronica guessed.

"What land are they *kumming* from?" Rose asked.

"I can show you on *Dat's* map later. It's Ontario, Canada. It takes maybe two days' drive to get here," Veronica explained.

"You mean they'll take the buggy all that way?" Rose asked horrified at the prospect.

"No, heavens, they'll get a driver. Maybe share the van with another family heading south."

"And what did they name her again?" Rose wanted to know.

"Isabella. I guess they could call her Izzy then," Veronica answered.

"I like them little like that. They don't try to bite you or run away on you. And they look like little burritos when they're all wrapped up snug. So sweet, eh?" Rose said.

"Ya. They are such a gift. A miracle, each one," Veronica said. She could still picture the last time she saw her own baby Marta at the funeral. So tiny, though she weighed five pounds, amazingly big for a preemie. Dressed in her little white dress. Absolutely perfect, except she wasn't living. *Oh! How my arms ached to hold her* chust *once more,* Veronica remembered. Of course, her eyes stung with the tears pooling there. *This one can't die too,* she thought, fear creeping into her mind and heart. *Dear* Gott, *please, please keep this one safe. I can't go through that again. I'd die. Anything but that.* Chust *a healthy* bobbel *waiting the whole nine months. Please,* Yesus.

"Why don't we have a new *bobbel* of our own?" Rose demanded, shocking Veronica, though she knew perfectly well this day would come eventually, when Rose would ask.

"Well, it's up to *Gott* when the *bobbeli kumm,*" Veronica explained daubing her eyes with her handkerchief. She honked into it and quickly tucked it back into her pocket.

"I'm gonna go to the phone box right now and call Him and tell Him to send us a new *bobbel,*" Rose said, swinging her arms while marching toward the back door. Veronica ran after her, turning her around by the shoulders and took Rose to the sofa. She sat her on her lap and explained that you just don't call God. That prayer usually works even better to get what you want, though God might decide to say 'no,' if it isn't the best thing for you or the right time.

"I'm going to check on *zapper* now," Veronica excused herself as Rose again took up her vigil on the window seat, her faceless Amish doll, Rosemary, on her lap waiting for the guests also.

"The snowflakes on the windows look great, by the way," Veronica called back to Rose.

"I know," was the response. And then, less than two minutes later came a loud scream from the living room.

"THEY'RE HERE *MAMM*. THEY'RE REALLY HERE!" Veronica quickly untied her apron and throwing it over a chair in the kitchen, ran out to meet the van with Rose already racing ahead of her. Henry came out of the barn at the sound of a car and jogged the rest of the way from the barn when he realized who was visiting. His brother of all people. And all the way from Ontario.

It sounded more like a hog pen than a reunion with family what for all the squeals from the children. They hadn't seen each other since the wedding over six months ago when they'd returned together from Ontario. And then Milo and Edith's family were gone, just like that, leaving Henry, Rose, and Veronica on their own to set up house-keeping.

"Look how big you've gotten," Milo exclaimed hugging Rose.

"You're almost as tall as I am, Lester," Henry marveled.

"You look *gut*. But how are you feelin'?" Edith asked Veronica who frowned and quickly shook her head ever so slightly, signaling that this conversation would most definitely have to wait for later, far away from little ears. Then Veronica reinforced her answer by tightly closing her lips and miming that she was zipping them shut besides. And then throwing away the key. Edith got the message, loud and clear.

Rose was going from one cousin to the next, hugging them all. She had grown up with them after her mother died and Henry moved in with Milo's family. Rose, along with all of the children, thought she was just part of the kid herd, oblivious to the fact that most families don't usually have two dads and just one mother. Not until Henry and Veronica were married did the truth dawn on any of the children. It still felt like their little playmate had been forcibly wrenched away from them. They'd missed her terribly. Not a day went by when they didn't think about her.

Henry looked above all the little people and found Veronica. He shook his head when he realized she'd been in on the prank, knowing they were coming. He was obviously the only one who wasn't privy to this visit.

Having greeted each one of her cousins Rose walked back to Edith.

"Can I see her?" she asked reaching for the baby. Edith sat down on the stone wall by the flower bed next to the driveway and unwrapped little Isabella.

Gazing at the little one, Rose gasped. "She's so beautiful," she exclaimed reaching for the tiny hand. "She's holding my finger! She's strong," Rose said surprised that a baby could even do that.

"Can I hold her *Mamm?*"

"Let's go sit on the couch for that, eh?" Edith suggested.

But before she got up, she hugged Rose again and whispered in her ear, "Veronica is your *mamm* now. You can call me *aendi*." Rose nodded that she heard her words but couldn't quite grasp their meaning yet. Edith had been her *mamm* for as far back as she could remember and called her that along with all the other children in the family. She would have to ask Veronica about it later, she decided, filing it in her memory banks along with all the other unanswered questions moldering there.

"Supper's going to get cold, you all. Better *kumm* in," Veronica said as she attempted to move this party into the house. Finally, everyone was washed up and sitting at the table, happily visiting.

"*Patties down?*" Henry announced the silent prayer.

The second he cleared his throat, indicating that the prayer was over, the kitchen burst into bedlam with everyone talking at once.

"Veronica, you've made a feast. You didn't have to do all this," Edith said.

Rose answered, "Oh yes, we did. It was a surprise. *Dat* didn't know at all," she explained.

"Yummasetti! *Mamm,* it's my favorite. They made Yummasetti!" Lester looked like he was going to cry, he was so overcome.

"It's my favorite, too. That's why I told her to make it," Rose stated.

Milo looked at Henry who looked at Veronica. Finally, he said, "Gosh, Henry. When did that one grow up, anyway?"

"Four going on fourteen is what it's called," Henry replied sarcastically.

"For real," Milo answered shaking his head. "So much for submissive, docile *meedel,* I guess," he added.

The platters made the rounds until most of the food was gone.

"Does anyone have room for dessert?" Veronica asked. Immediately Rose dipped her head and covered her mouth with both hands. Veronica glared down at her and Rose immediately sat up straighter and assumed a more serious demeanor. She knew what was coming. This was going to be good.

"Sounds *gut* to me," Milo answered. The others agreed.

Henry asked, "What did you make?"

Veronica answered, "*Chust* taste it first."

"Oh, then I know what's *kumming*," he said ruefully.

"*Dat,* don't tell them," Rose told him across the table. The other children were genuinely astonished. No child in their house was allowed to correct or admonish a parent under any circumstance. Ever. Never. On pain of death.

"You'll have to guess," Veronica said. "Rose, please get the dessert plates out while I clear the table."

Edith passed Izzy to Milo and helped carry plates and platters to the sink while Veronica cut the large cake.

"Yum. I declare, that looks *erschtaunlich*," Milo pronounced.

"It's really *gut*," Rose said, chuckling as she brought a slice of the cake to each one at the table.

"May I have Izzy's piece, too?" Milo teased, making Rose giggle. "It looks really *gut*," he said.

Veronica served coffee then and sat down.

"This is really *gut*," Edith remarked. "What's in it, Veronica?"

"Well, Maudie had it in *The Budget* this past week. It's called, Pork and Beans cake," she said, knowing that by divulging this piece of information she could set off a major rebellion.

"Aw, *yucke!*" Lester shouted, throwing his fork down on the table where it landed with a clunk.

"Lester, your manners!" his father shouted back, stunned

at his son's behavior. Then he looked at Veronica and asked, "Is it really?"

"Yes, it really is," Veronica said and laughed out loud.

Edith studied a bite on her fork, frowning. "It tastes okay. How is it made then?"

"I don't care for mine now," Abby, who was seven years old said politely as she pushed her plate away.

"Me, too," copied Ruby who was five and did everything Abby did. Leonard, four-years old, kept eating, the icing mainly. He always ate the icing first. Louie, who just turned two and was strapped into a highchair, was oblivious to everything going on around him. He simply kept eating, with his hands.

Henry was enjoying this immensely. "Tomorrow *nacht* we're having Dirt Pudding," he announced which riled the troops even more.

Abby gagged, causing her mother to jump up from her chair and hold an empty bowl under her chin should she decide to lose her supper right then and there at the table.

Edith turned to Henry. "Do you mind? Maybe not at the table," she scolded him.

Turning to face Veronica, Edith said, "That's not really funny."

"Yes, it is," Rose corrected Edith, laughing.

"Don't you correct me, Missy," Edith warned.

"Sorry, *Mamm*," Rose apologized. Then she revised her answer. "I mean *Aendi*."

A minute later Rose announced, "There are gummy worms in Dirt Pudding."

We are known by our actual deeds and not by what we boast that we can do.
- Amish school motto

CHAPTER 13
Honey Pies

"We should visit Eli and Hazel today, *liebling*. What do you think?" Veronica posed the idea at second breakfast a few days later.

"Oh, yes, *Mamm*. Can we bring them some leftover cake...and some coffee filter snowflakes for their windows? They'd like that," Rose answered, nodding once in confirmation.

"*Gut*, then. Let's finish up cleaning, hang out the wash and then we can go," Veronica planned. Just then Henry appeared in the kitchen doorway.

"Any chance of a warmup? Any *kaffi* left over from breakfast?" he asked holding up his to-go mug.

"Oh, sure," Veronica answered taking the thermos. Before she could say anything else their little chatterbox informed him, "We're gonna bring some cake to Eli and Hazel and some snowflakes, too."

"Well," Henry began. "You'll be hard pressed to find any snowflakes this time of year. I reckon it'll be at least a couple of months yet...."

"No, silly," Rose insisted. "We'll cut them outta coffee

filters, like ours," she said pointing to the kitchen windows which were covered in 'snowflakes.'

"Oh, I get it," Henry played along.

"Here's your *kaffi,* honey pie. We'll be home for supper," Veronica told him.

"*Pennsylfaani denki,*" Rose requested.

"There are some grownup conversations not meant for little ears," Henry said firmly.

"I know, I know," Rose pouted. Then perking up she asked, "But what's a honey pie anyway? Can we make one for Eli?" The grownups laughed at that.

"Maybe," Veronica answered.

"There's no such thing," Henry explained. "It's *chust* a term of endearment, it means you love someone, like 'sweetheart' or 'darling.'"

"Oh, like you call *Mamm?*" Rose asked.

Veronica hesitated. Without correcting her husband in front of Rose, she tentatively offered, "Well, someone actually did *kumm* up with a honey pie, and when I was a teacher, I came across some obscure trivia and found that in 1796 someone named Samuel Coleridge first wrote it in a letter."

"Probably a *liebesbreif* to his honey," Rose added laughing.

"How would you possibly know about *liebesbreifs?*" Henry demanded, completely disarmed by a four-and-a-half-year-old-almost-five-year-old child.

"Well, Lester told me that Valentine's Day was 'bout writing love letters to your sweethearts, but you didn't have to actually *marry* whoever you sent a Valentine's Day card to," she explained. "They always made the cards at school. I'll be in school next year, right?"

"Well, I never...." Henry marveled, frowning and shaking his head.

"I think maybe we should make a honey pie for Eli and Hazel," Veronica suggested.

"Oh, yes!" Rose said clapping and jumping up and down like a spring lamb which she did often.

"I'll look in Lovina's cookbook. Maybe she's got it," Veronica said. "At least one of my cookbooks will have it."

"If that's the case, then perhaps you'd better make one for your own honey pie, too, *Mamm*," Henry suggested with a wink which thankfully Rose didn't see but was clear as day to Veronica.

"Oh yes, *Mamm*. Two pies?" Rose begged. "Please?"

Henry returned to the horses in the paddocks while Veronica and Rose went to work. They tidied the bedrooms and cleaned and refilled the lamps. You don't want to leave kerosene lamps with smoky glass chimneys and little fuel for later in the day. You want them ready for the evening, by dusk at the very latest.

There was a knock at the front door. They stopped what they were doing and looked at each other. No one knocked at the front door. Ever. At least not any *Amische* did. It had to be an *Englischer*.

"I'm not expecting anyone," Veronica said wiping her hands on her apron as she walked to the door, checking that her *kapp* was on straight as she went.

"Just sign here," a man dressed in brown requested when she opened the door. Veronica could see the UPS truck still running on idle in the driveway. Rose watched this encounter from behind her *mamm's* skirt. Veronica signed and exchanged the clipboard for the package with the driver.

"Thank you, ma'am," the man said as he turned and

jogged back to his truck. As soon as he was out of earshot Rose said excitedly,

"He called you *'mamm' Mamm*, why did that man *chust* call you *'mamm'*?"

"It's *chust* a polite way the *Englischers* talk. It doesn't mean 'mom' or 'mother' to them," she explained.

"Huh," Rose said to herself. *Englischers* could be a strange bunch, for sure. Then she turned her attention to the package.

"What is it?" she asked.

"Why, I don't know. Not a clue. Can you get me the Exacto knife from the kitchen drawer? We'll see what this is. I don't remember ordering anything..." she said as she read the return address label aloud. "Huh. Holmes Brooms, Township Road, Millersburg, Ohio," she muttered to herself. "Huh. No clue."

"Hurry, *Mamm*. What is it?" Rose asked as Veronica carefully cut open the package.

"Maybe something *Dat* ordered," Veronica wondered.

When the last sheet of brown paper and bubble wrap was removed, she looked at the little broom.

"Well, I think this is for you," Veronica said smiling, and handed the brand-new child-size corn straw broom to Rose.

She was dumbfounded. While examining the small broom, a smile slowly formed on her lips. Then she proceeded to try it out, sweeping in a little circle in the great room. Yessiree. It was her very own, first-ever broom. Then she attacked her task with a vengeance swinging right and left, dispersing any dust there to the four corners of the room.

"Whoa, there. Settle down. Let me show you once." Veronica gently took the little broom from Rose and demonstrated the mechanics of sweeping.

"I'll have to tell *Dat* I swept the *die gut shtup*, eh?" Rose asked, her pride glowing.

"Yes, you are doing *chust* that, my *liebling*," Veronica said tearing up. *And I suppose I will cry too on her first day of school.*

"Oh, *denki, Mamm. Denki*," Rose said, her face flushed with happiness.

"Well, I'm guessing this is a gift from your *Dat*. You'll have to thank him" Veronica said, and then thought to herself, *I* chust *hope he wasn't planning to save this for a* Grischtdaag *gift.*

"Okay," Veronica announced. "Time to start those pies, my little honey." Rose laughed and answered, "Okay, my big honey."

Snowflakes are such fragile things but look what happens when they stick together.
~ Amish proverb

CHAPTER 14

Snap Peas Wars

Veronica steered the horse and buggy off the macadam shoulder and onto a long dirt road lined with trees.

"What's the surprise?" Rose wanted to know.

"*Chust* you be patient," her mother said.

"Would ya look at that garden!" Rose exclaimed as they drove past a field lined with row after row of plants, most looking lush and quite ready to pick. There were numerous vegetables, and rows of flowers in between the rows of vegetables. Blueberry bushes, black raspberry bushes, currants, grape vines on sturdy trellises, and a row of plum trees circled the perimeter. The air was nippy, but fall was often like that. A fine mist had started while they were on their way. Veronica pointed out the paddock beyond the kitchen garden dotted with horses, cows and then...what was that? Rose recognized that one from her picture book they'd picked up recently from the town library.

"*Mamm! Maaaaaaam!*" she shouted, standing up from the buggy bench and gripping the dashboard, while leaning out through the windshield. "*Mamm!*...it's a zebra! And there are ostriches, and look! Llamas, too. And...and is this place a zoo? I never gone to a zoo. *Mamm?*"

Well, you could call it that, what with ten kinner, Veronica thought to herself. *I can't imagine....*

Then to Rose, "Not really, but they have a whole host of exotic animals. It's become quite a lucrative business, uh, that means they are making enough money doing this. I heard that a full-grown single mating pair of alpacas can fetch as much as $35,000. Rose, that's more than all our animals put together. It's a lot of money." Then Veronica thought to herself, *I think maybe we're in the wrong business. Hm, now that's an idea...*and then as an afterthought she added, *camels? Elephants? We could charge admission....*

Veronica drove the horse up to the gate at the paddock, noticing the clothes lines on that side of the house. Impossibly long lines reached from a post at the paddock gate to pullies secured above the porch by the kitchen door. A girl could be seen, well, in truth only her feet and the hem of her burgundy dress, below a sheet she was clipping to the line. A dozen pairs of barndoor trousers standing like soldiers lined up were pinned to the lines, too. On the next line, already, hung cloth diapers, at least a couple dozen of them, flapping in the wind like flags at the United Nations. The next line sported shirts—white, blue, green, lavender. All homemade, from small to extra-large. On the last line were the dresses, all hung in order, as if graded from small to large. Greens, blues, teal, lavender, rose, plum, and black, with matching pinafores, capes and aprons. A drying spider hung from a hook on the porch with a dozen pairs of plastic pants pinned to its spokes.

Veronica shook her head while gazing at so many lines of washing. "*Heavens, that's a lot of washing. Wonder if ours will ever look like that. Golly,*" was what she was thinking.

Josiah had heard them coming in and jogged through the yard to where they were.

"Hi, there," he greeted them. "Great to see you."

"Those are zebras!" Rose jumped in. She'd been spoken to, so this was allowed, she figured, while she was instructed that children were to be seen and not heard, but now he had addressed her. Right?

Veronica looked down at Rose with 'that look.' It was unmistakable. She stopped talking.

"Yup, they are. And who are you?" Josiah asked.

"I'm Rose. I'm almost five," she rushed to tell him, since she was relatively sure she'd been spoken to properly this time.

"And I have a calf and we're making stuff for Christmas," she rattled on until Veronica placed her hand a little bit firmer than usual on Rose's shoulder which put the lid on that conversation right quick.

"Well, *kumm* inside. We're having dinner in a bit. Can you stay?" he inquired.

"That would be nice," Veronica answered. "*Denki.*"

They followed him to the kitchen door, accompanied that far by a yappy little beagle. Rose bent down to scratch behind his ear.

"*Mamm,* can we get a dog? Please?" she asked.

"We'll ask *Dat,*" was all Veronica would commit to.

As they entered the kitchen through the back door Veronica surveyed the huge room, her first thought thinking it would be quite a jog from the sink across the vast floor to get to the gigantic cookstove. The room was relatively quiet, anyone speaking at all kept it to a low hum. Then as the company came in, despite everyone being there, even that died down to nothing, only the little pops from the wood burning in the cookstove fire box could be heard, two pea shuckers sitting in the middle of the floor, stifling their giggles while supposedly shucking peas. Truth was they were throwing as many peas at each other as they were dropping into the bowl sitting between them.

The blue curtains were tied back. There were Mason jars of wildflowers on a shelf by the stove and at a smaller side table. Dandelions drooped completely over their jar rims, not having agreed to flourish away from the great outdoors. The cattails, wild yarrow, and black-eyed Susans appeared oblivious to their new surroundings, though. Above a long rack with hat pegs which sported both their Sunday black dress hats and the everyday wheat straw hats, trophies from their hunting endeavors were proudly displayed, too. The deer antlers lined up next to each other there spanning that whole side of the room, representing at least a decade of successful hunts.

The extra-long old oak table was a hive of activity. There were children everywhere. Stacks of store-bought Christmas cards were sitting in the center of the table. There were children on both sides of the table signing cards before shoving them down the line to the next one tasked with putting them in the envelopes. The cards then progressed down the table to the child licking the envelopes before sending the cards on to the last one on the bench who would stick on the stamps.

In the middle of the floor sat two younger ones, maybe seven and eight-years-old or so with a large stainless-steel bowl between them and a five-gallon bucket of peas to be shelled. The pods were added to another bucket after they'd given up their peas. The two children tried their best to stifle their giggles, but embarrassed to be sitting on the floor with company watching them was too much. Their job wasn't finished, so they knew they couldn't just get up and hide somewhere.

An older girl with a forest green outfit and blue bandana over her hairs stood at the cookstove in her cooking apron, stirring a large pot while another girl, also with her apron on over a lovely Dutch blue dress, her *kapp* neatly pinned in place, was washing up the dishes at the sink and stacking them to air dry.

An older boy was draped over a rocking chair by the living room doorway, oblivious to all the activity, who was obviously catching a nap, probably having been up for barn chores hours before the others. His faded barndoor trousers were patched. His suspenders hanging over the armrests. His light blue shirt practically begged to be washed.

He'd be up and feeding the animals in another hour. The tasks were endless. At least the cows had been milked. That took the longest task of everything on the to-do list. He'd still muck out the stalls, loading the straw and manure into a wagon which would be hitched up to one of the donkeys later to haul into the rye field which would be disked and made ready for the next crop after it fertilized the ground there. Rotating crops was work but well worth it when you saw the superior produce coming in that the rich soil was able to provide.

Tip toeing silently around him was another girl sweeping escaped peas in the direction back toward the shelling project. There were several peas dotting the floor, having been participants in a game that included lobbing peas at your opponent.

A calico cat wandered into the kitchen from the living room and was swiftly scooped up and escorted outside by another girl who had just finished washing her hairs in the chore sink by the mud room. In one deft move she threw a towel over her dripping hairs and grabbed the cat before tossing it outside, through the screen door which shut back into place with a bang.

Three bushel baskets of apples were on the floor by the sink. They would soon be transformed into *schnitz,* or dried apples—the whole lot of them—which would keep nicely in jars throughout the coming year. Apple pies, main dishes, chutneys and jams, and pancakes, to name a few, would include *schnitz.* A little card table on the other side of the room was filled with gleaming glass quart jars of peaches in syrup, canned only the day before and left out to cool before being transported to join the others in the root cellar. You could see a single peach pit in each jar if you looked for it. Home canning experts have included the pits —only one pit per jar, mind you—for scores of years, claiming they help the peaches retain their glistening color.

Esther conducted it all from her post near the stove, giving the young sous-chef there suggestions as she spiced the chili. A chunky toddler was positioned on Esther's hip. You couldn't tell if he was a boy, or in fact a girl by what he or she was wearing. A beige muslin dress didn't necessarily mean the child was a girl. Amish boys wear the same standard baby dress until they are potty trained, usually. It is so much easier to change babies' diapers without having all the zippers and buttons or snaps that little boys' store-bought pants and overalls contain.

Looks like another little dishwasher or woodchopper is on the way, too, Veronica thought to herself. That is how the Amish announce a new baby's arrival to their families and friends. *How does she manage?* Veronica wondered in awe of it all. At that moment Veronica noticed Esther eyeing her own protruding tummy. Then their eyes met. Esther was smiling. Veronica nodded ever so slightly back at her, a universal unspoken sign that her suspicions were correct. Josiah came in after seeing to Veronica's buggy. He headed straight toward the chore sink and washed up there.

Esther announced then that it was time to get dinner out. The two pea shooters continued giggling while sending one last volley of peas each flying across the floor before picking up the buckets and bowls and depositing them by the dry sink.

Rose walked up to the two children and asked, "Do your pigs eat the skins?"

The little boy answered. "Yes, but we get the peas. *Mamm* cans 'em." His little sister nodded her agreement, and then added, "and freezes 'em too." The girl with the broom followed them and swept the most recently deployed peas into her dustpan without a word. The card project at the table was quickly packed up and moved on trays over to a long sideboard along one wall in the kitchen. The junior sous-chef was lifting a giant round cast iron skillet from the oven with two hot mitts, placing it on the right side of the stove top to cool.

Then, as instructed by her mother, the little assistant chef threw a clean dish towel over the corn bread so it would sweat and stay soft. The table was wiped, places set, and water poured into glasses. Soup bowls were stacked at the end of the table by the stove from where Esther could fill them. The corn bread was cut and arranged on two plat-ters, each one placed on opposite ends of the long table, and a jar of maple syrup was placed there next to a block of fresh-churned butter on a pie plate. Another block of butter sat at the other end of the table. The toddler was strapped into his highchair then and a generous bib tied on. He commenced swinging his legs which almost but not quite touched the tabletop. Scooting his bottom down in the highchair as far as the straps would allow, he tried again, this time able to catch the very edge of the table with his toes. He smiled then, obviously very proud of his prowess.

When everyone was finally seated, Josiah bowed his head after asking, *"Patties down?"* Instantly all hands, (and toes) from the largest to the tiniest, were whisked under the table, (and highchair tray.) After a silent prayer, he cleared his throat and addressed Veronica.

"After we eat, we'd love to take you on tour of the zoo. That's what we're calling it now."

Veronica put on her most sober face and asked, "When are you getting an elephant? I've never seen a real live one. Wouldn't you like an elephant?" Little heads silently nodded around the table, mouths chewing the wonderful dinner.

Veronica continued. "And maybe some alligators?"

"Some animals are more acclimated to tropical climates and here we are in the Midwest with snow and subzero temperatures," he answered. "But I don't know if anyone has tried alligators yet."

Everyone laughed then. Josiah went on to tell them about the animals, where he got them from and the state of rescued circus animals in North America.

"It's even worse in Europe. Many of the animals there are abused and neglected. There are groups trying to ban *any* animals in circuses. Here in the states, they're not doing a bad job, but it could be better," he explained.

Then Esther asked, "Veronica, you and I are related somehow. Third cousins once removed or something, maybe? Anyway, it's great to see you. That wedding was beautiful."

Rose, seated next to her, leaned into Veronica and whispered in her ear. "Am I related then too? Are they all more cousins?"

"Yes, you are. We better get out the family tree book and bring it all up to date, I'm thinking," Veronica suggested. Then Rose leaned in once more and whispered behind her hand. "What are all their names?" she wanted to know.

Veronica explained, "We are wondering what all your names are."

Josiah washed down his last mouthful of chili and said, "Oh, that's easy. I'll start here and we'll go around the table. I'm Josiah. I'm thinking I'm the *dat* here," he said, thought a minute and then added, "actually, my title is 'head zookeeper,' I'm thinking," which was met with peals of laughter.

Then the teenage girl next to him said, "I'm Philomena. I'm sixteen." And around the table it went. The only child not named was busy carefully picking out kidney beans from his plastic Peter Rabbit bowl and popping them in his mouth. Josiah answered for him. "That's Ezra."

So, they were Josiah, Philomena, Ezra, Luke, Simon, Greta, Heather, Katie, Pennelope, Vera, Phoebe, and Esther. *And another one on the way,* Veronica thought to herself, *how in heaven's name do they manage? They're all so gut. Bright, happy, obedient kinner. Dear Lord, please teach us Your ways. Please be with us and give us wisdom, patience and the right kind of love.*

Advent is a short season, but it is the long road of a soul from Nazareth to Bethlehem. It is such a short distance as we are accustomed to thinking of distances. Yet it is a road into infinity, into eternity, having a beginning, but no end.
~ C. D.

CHAPTER 15

If Cows Could Talk

Veronica and Rose were in the barn helping Henry finish up the evening milking. Each had a little milking stool. Veronica and Rose shared a cow, each positioning their three-legged stool on either side of the same cow. Henry worked faster and could milk two cows by himself in the same amount of time it took Veronica and Rose to milk just one.

"*Mamm,* do you think cows talk to each other when we're not around?" Rose asked while still milking their cow.

"They might talk in cow language, like birds and other animals, pigs, I suppose," she responded. *What all must go through that girl's mind,* Veronica thought to herself. *Whatever next?*

"But what if we could understand them?" she continued. "Do you think we ever could? Maybe if we hide in the barn at *nacht?*"

"I don't think we would understand it," Veronica said pondering that, "uh-uh."

"What do you reckon they about in their cow language then?" Rose asked.

"I suppose the other animals, their baby cows maybe, or food. Nice grass in the field, ya know," Veronica guessed, quite entertained by this discussion.

Henry had been listening to this exchange with amusement. "I read a while back in a dairy magazine called the *Small Farmer's Journal*, that cows have been found to regularly talk to each other about food and the weather in their own language, according to a study by a bunch of scientists in Sydney, Australia. They swear that they discovered that each cow has its own individual moo and can change its pitch depending on how they are feeling."

"Hm. I wonder how much funding went into that research, eh?" Veronica mused. "That was probably enough money to feed a whole town in India for a year."

"Maybe," Rose began again, "if I talk to my calf enough, like every day, maybe she'll learn our language from me and we could talk together, ya think?"

"You could try, but I don't know if that'd work," Henry offered.

"Or I could move into the barn and learn cow talk from them," Rose pondered sounding hopeful.

Then Veronica spoke. "Well, Rose, there is a very old Norwegian legend that says that every *Grischtdaagnacht* the animals are able to talk to each other and they all understand. I'll read it to you tonight for your bedtime story, ya? I've got the book," she added. Rose's eyes were as big as saucers then. "Oh, yes, *Mamm!* Please," she agreed.

"But is it true?" she asked suddenly frowning.

"Well, legends come from long ago times, so we're not sure who started them and if they saw these things themselves. We can only wonder," Veronica said.

Later that night Veronica found the book hidden among her treasures in the cedar chest her own *Dat* had built for her as a wedding gift when she married Amos. *Dat* had not lived long enough to witness her marriage to Henry. She ran her hand over the lid of the cedar chest as she closed it, thinking fondly of her dear *Dat*.

"A Christmas Eve Legend by Marion Dame Bauer," Veronica began. Rose had bathed and was tucked into bed. Veronica was stretched out next to her on top of the quilt with the open book on her chest so that Rose could follow the pictures.

"At first, the animals refused to allow the humans into the manger, as they looked down on them and their behavior. But, the animals relent, and Mary and Joseph are allowed into the stable for the *nacht*," Veronica read.

"*Mamm*, what is 'relent'?" Rose wanted to know. Veronica translated as best she could. Rose was learning English in record time, but some words still eluded her. Veronica continued to read.

"Suddenly the manger is showered with light from the Star of Bethlehem" she read quite dramatically.

"That *nacht,* as Jesus is born, the animals are overwhelmed with love for each other, even the hogs are allowed into the stable for the first time *chust* to see the Baby."

Rose stopped Veronica from reading on. "Do you think there were even cats and their *glieder,* too, *Mamm?*"

"Well, it does say 'all the animals' so I'd say yes, even the cats and their kittens."

Veronica continued. "Then, the animals come to the realization that they have been given the gift of speech to tell the world of the Miracle, the birth of Christ. However, as they run through Bethlehem, each animal loses his gift. They return to the stable in silence, but with newfound respect and love for each other. The ox, the last one to lose his speech, is left to wonder if humanity will ever understand the miracle that has been given. Long ago and even today, the story is told of how all the animals in the world, at the stroke of midnight on Christmas Eve, speak. Before they lose their newfound power of speech, the animals rejoice at the birth of Jesus, born humbly in a manger and surrounded by animals."

Rose was soon asleep, already dreaming about talking to her little calf who could talk back. So was Veronica. Henry closed up the barn and returned to the house. He made the rounds that he walked every night, blowing out the lamps, checking the wood stoves, closing the dampers and getting ready for bed. He found Veronica sound asleep next to Rose. Gently removing the book, he patted her hand and whispered, *"Kumm* to bed, my love." Soon they were all asleep. It had been a *gut* day. A blessed day.

Prepare an inn internally, every day, for the Child to be born in, the Child who was denied an inn and who still is denied the inns of many hearts.
~ C.D.

CHAPTER 16
Canada or Bust

"What 'cha doin' *Dat?*" Rose wanted to know after watching him for a couple of minutes, intrigued by the meticulous task he was performing at the kitchen table.

"I'm making some of my lures, *daumling,*" Henry explained. "I fish with them. The fish think they're real bugs and go after them and then, *ou la,* they're caught."

"Wah-what?" Rose asked.

"That's French for, uh, well, 'there you are,'" Henry said.

"And you grew up in Ontario talking French, right?" she asked.

"*Oui, mademoiselle,*" he agreed. Then, as an afterthought he added, "Why don't you *chust* learn English first? Then we can work on your French later, eh?"

"*Oui,*" she agreed, with a sly little grin. "But why would you wanna catch fish when it's almost winter, *Dat,* why?"

"I'm making them for a *Grischtdaag* gift for my *bruder* Milo. How would you like to spend *Ztvett Grischtdaag* with your cousins in Milverton?" he added nonchalantly.

"WHAT? REALLY?" she squeaked. In another second

86

she was racing out to the clothes lines where Veronica was hanging the wash.

"*Mamm! MAMM! Dat* says we're going to Canada for *Ztvett Grischtdaag,*" she screeched as the kitchen door slammed behind her with a thud.

Once she was standing there next to Veronica, she frowned, suddenly becoming quite solemn. "Are we *really* or is he *chust* teasing me again or is it true?" she demanded, her arms folded in front of her, the frown frozen in place along with an unmistakable pout.

"We'd really like to go, *daumling.*" Veronica confirmed. "We'd like to celebrate *Grischtdaag* here with our family and then go up to Ontario to be with *Dat's* side of the family for *Zrvett Grischtdaag.*"

"How come we have it two times? How will we know which one the animals will talk for? If we're in Canada, we'll miss them here. I really want to hear my little calf talk, *Mamm,*" Rose said as she began to tear up. She sniffed and swiped her arm across her eyes.

The conversation continued at supper that night.

"I don't want to miss Charlotte talking," Rose explained once again. And again, the tears came right on cue.

"Where did you get that name from anyway?" Henry asked, totally mystified.

"You mean Charlotte? It's from the book *Mamm* read to me, *Charlotte's Web,*" Rose explained.

"Huh. Really? Okay," Henry marveled.

"Charlotte is a she, isn't she?" Rose asked.

"Why, yes. She will grow up to be a proper milk cow," Veronica explained.

"Well, *darr,*" Henry said as he attempted to assuage his

daughter's tears, "If it is while we're here, *gut*. If it happens instead at *Ztvett Grischtdaag*, then maybe you'll be in *Onkel* Milo's barn and their animals will be talking there. *Chust* maybe." *Boy, now what have I gotten myself into?* he asked himself.

"But *Mamm*, why are there two? *Grischtdaags?*" Rose pushed on.

"Well, see, there is the night baby *Yesus* was born, the most holy night of *Grischtdaag*, and then the Kings came to visit—I guess it took them awhile to find the manger. They only had the star to go by but when they finally made it, they brought Him gifts later at *Ztvett Grischtdaag* so we share gifts that day, not so much on His birthday."

"Huh," Rose responded. It was all a bit much to understand. All she was concerned about just now was getting to hear her little calf talk. She'd been practicing with her every day in the barn. As far as she was concerned, she was getting nowhere fast.

The next week was a blur of activity: gifts to finish making and wrap. Cookies and pies to make for the guests who will be coming to visit over Christmas, and more pies and cookies to bring along to all the families that had invited the little family to visit them over Christmas.

Veronica wanted the house *redded* up before any visitors came for Christmas and planned on giving it a once-over again before their trip to Milverton. It was the worst thing to come home to a messy house after a long journey when you are too tired to tackle it all.

Henry had already enlisted the help of the Ech boys to come for the chores morning and evening while they would be away. They would also keep a small fire going in the basement wood stove so the temperature in the house wouldn't meet the minus twenty degrees or more marks that were predicted for the coming weeks outside. There were pipes connecting the gravity water system that ran into the main kitchen. There were close to a hundred canning jars in the root cellar representing a whole harvest from the kitchen garden. If those freeze, they could easily burst—an absolutely catastrophic event no one wanted to even think about, much less clean up.

And then there were the shelves of squashes: Hubbards, acorns, butternut, buttercup, spaghetti, Costata Romanesco, delicata, honey nut, kabocha, patty pan, carnival squash, turban squash, Kabosha, and cousa. Veronica decided earlier that year to explore all the different types of squashes and ordered seeds for them all from Seed Savers Exchange based in Arkansas, Wisconsin. Because all of the squash was organic and considered heirlooms, she could also harvest the seeds herself and share them with others, keeping back enough of a supply for her to use the next year. There were also potatoes, onions and kohlrabies, turnips, pumpkins, rutabagas, carrots and parsnips buried in sand in the wood box in the root cellar next to the sixty-gallon sauerkraut crock. The dill pickle barrel was also happily fermenting down there. All would keep till Spring, unless they too froze inadvertently. Any leftover food had to be sealed in mouse-proof containers in the kitchen pantry upstairs. Nothing must be left out for any hungry little rodents scouting out the meager offerings there. Tin cans worked well for that.

Back home, when Veronica was just a teen, the family left for just two days to go visiting for Christmas and upon returning home, found teeth marks on every single Tupperware container in the house. The cereal bins, the butter keeper, the pie containers, the bread box—there were even tiny teeth marks all the way around the round lid of the plastic apple cider vinegar jug, as if the mice could smell the contents in each container. But vinegar? *Dat* set traps and for a full week after that they caught as many as eleven mice a day (the children kept count on a tally sheet in the kitchen) until one day when they didn't catch any. Obviously, word had gotten out that this farm was no longer an option for the rodent populations in that county. Perhaps, like the Travelers, also known as gypsies or Roma depending on what country you live in, the mice left a chalk mark by the front gate warning any and all that this was *not* a good house to visit.

"What 'cha doin' *Dat?*" Rose asked as she leaned into him and wrapped her arms around his neck. He was sitting at the sewing machine in the bright eastern guest bedroom where Veronica had set up her sewing room.

"Are you sewing?" she asked incredulously. "What are ya makin'?" she continued.

"I didn't know *dats* could sew. Did yer *mamm* teach you? My *mamm* said she would teach me. Did ya know?" she kept asking.

"Well," Henry said between her barrage of questions.

"No, I don't sew but I do know how to clean and repair machines, but today I am building up an extension on the foot pedal of this one," he answered.

"Why? *Dat,* what is a 'tension? Huh?" she continued.

"Well," he patiently explained. "Your feet don't reach the floor yet. The way this machine is made is for taller *fraus,* not little *meedels.* I'm measuring this block so I can cut it to fit the foot plate here. Then I can screw it down and you can try it out."

"Who? Me? *Mmmm?* Ahhh...really? Why?" she stuttered.

"Cause your tibia is actually only nine inches long and this sewing machine was built for a grownup's leg length," he mumbled as he held up the tape measure one more time, then bumped his head on the cabinet as he tried to unfold himself from underneath it.

"Gotcha!" he said triumphantly as he first stretched his shoulders and then stood up, reading the tape measure one last time, just to be sure, causing Rose to startle.

"Why me, huh *Dat?*" she repeated her question.

Henry grabbed Rose by her waist and lifted her up into a hug.

"Because someday, I hope not too soon, mind you, you'll need to know how to sew for your *halsband* and *kinner,* that's why." That left Rose completely befuddled.

"What *halsband?*" she finally asked. "I married you and Veronica," she reasoned.

"Oh, dear," he laughed. Then to himself, *I think it might be time for one of our little talks.*

When did she grow up? And we'll have another one soon. Yikes. Now I know why that old guy at the horse auction told me that you should never outnumber yourselves. 'Twos the limit' he said, and I can barely keep up with one.

"Well then, maybe you can talk to your *mamm* about it sometime," he said, having decided to divert the conundrum to her realm.

Rose continued to puzzle. "So, when do we go?"

"You mean to Canada?" he asked. She nodded her head.

"Well, the day after *Grischtdaag,* or maybe the next after that. It'll be here before we know it," he added.

"And you'll teach me how to sew first?" she asked.

"Whoa. No. Your *mamm* will teach you how to sew," he corrected her.

"But you'll teach me how to make fishing lures, eh?" she said.

"Well, I guess I could. Yeah."

Advent is a time of waiting to be forgiven, and a time of knowing that I am forgiven. It is a strange combining of old and the new, as if eons of waiting, mankind's waiting, have suddenly entered my soul.
~ C.D.

Part Two

You are welcome
Here be at your ease
Get up when you are ready
Go to bed when you please
Happy to share with you
Such as we've got
The leaks in the roof
The soups in the pot.
You don't have to thanks us
Or laugh at our jokes
Sit down and come often
You are one of the folks.

Found hand lettered on a wooden plaque in a guest room where the author recently stayed at an Amish farm.

CHAPTER 17

A Mother's Worst Fear

Before bed, Veronica read once more the offering for the day given by her little calendar. It always brought peace. Tonight was no different.

To me, prayer has always been a matter of listening...in the midst of the turmoil around me, this inner listening brings peace. - C. D.

She breathed in a sigh of relief and turned the page so it would be ready first thing in the morning. She knelt by the bed silently saying her prayers before crawling under the quilt. Henry would be back soon after checking the barn.

It had been a good day. A peaceful day. A blessed day. Her last words before falling asleep were, *"denki, Gott. Denki."*

Veronica sat straight up in bed and listened for a minute. There. There it was again. She got up, turned on her flashlight and ran into the next bedroom following the raucous cough. Rose was thrashing around in bed, her cheeks bright red while she continued coughing. Veronica lit the Coleman lamp on the dresser, scooped Rose up and sat on the bed rocking her.

"There, there," she cooed. "So, what is this?" she asked. Totally drained, Rose leaned against Veronica, gasping for breath.

"Where would you pick up something like this?" Veronica asked. The child in her lap didn't respond. She didn't look up either. *Edith's visit,* Veronica remembered. *I wonder if they have it, too? Get Henry to call them later. Ya, that would be* gut. And then the terrible, awful thought came to her. Would whatever this is affect their baby, especially if she was in her first trimester? *Dear* Gott, *I am putting all of this in Your Hands. Help us* Yesus! *Please...*

"I'm going to call your *dat* in here," Veronica told the limp little body in her arms before shouting for Henry who came into the room rubbing his eyes and squinting at her.

"She's really sick. Fever and an awful cough. This isn't *chust* the flu or something, Henry. What do we do?" she asked, the fear in her voice palpable. "She's barely conscious, Henry."

Then Veronica thought to herself, *okay, calm down. Get the fever down first. Maybe it isn't that bad.*

"Why don't you get the dishpan and fill it with water from the spigot, that'll be cool—half full—and get a handful of washcloths. We'll try to get the fever down first." Henry was fully awake now and could feel Veronica's fear in the room; you could cut it with a knife. He ran to get the dishpan of water and coming back up the stairs brought it in and held it for Veronica. Then she took off Rose's night-gown and squeezing out a rag, began rubbing her down. The awful squeaky cough continued. After a few minutes Rose appeared to doze off.

"She's almost floppy, Henry. What could it be? I don't know what to do," she said, ready to panic.

Then Henry asked, "How 'bout I'll make some of that Throat Coat herbal tea and we can spoon it into her? It might help," Henry offered.

"I don't know a thing about childhood diseases. What do we do then? What if it doesn't help? Oh, Henry, I can't lose another *bobbel. I chust* can't. I can't lose her, Henry," she burst into tears, hugging Rose to herself.

"I'm making tea. You wait here, okay?" Henry said, taking charge of the situation. The coughing continued. Rose's whole chest was wracked with each cough, as she gasped for air. Veronica could hear the creaky stairs as Henry hurried down to the kitchen, two steps at a time.

She prayed, harder than she'd ever prayed, if that were at all possible. She felt as if she was falling into a black abyss, despairing even of His help now.

Here Gott, *my first baby died, and I thought the world had ended. Then you took Amos. But then You sent Henry. And Rose, who was the icing on the cake. I realized You had indeed dried every tear. But I couldn't bear it if You took Rose too, now. Please don't, please help us. Please Gott...*

Finally, Henry returned to the bedroom. "I put in a tad of lemon juice and honey. Here, I think it is cool enough," he said as he crouched down next to the bed and offered a teaspoon of the tea from a cup to Rose. He dribbled it into her mouth and waited to see if she'd swallowed it.

"What should we do now?" Veronica pleaded desperately.

"Well, it's five o'clock in the morning. I'm thinking I go get that nurse and bring her here. She might have the best advice for us," Henry suggested.

"Ya. You do that. *Gut* idea. *Chust* hurry, Henry," Veronica begged. "Phoebe Schwartz. Her name is Phoebe

Schwartz. I think they live near the bulk food store. Ya, that's it."

"I'll be back soon, okay? It'll be alright. You'll see." Henry tried to assure Veronica, though he wasn't sure that it would be okay. Not at all.

Phoebe had earned her nursing license four years ago. The bishops in the surrounding districts had met and decided to ask if she would be willing to go to community college in order to be able to help out at home with all the innumerable needs of the families there. The LPN nursing program was a two-year course. When she got there, she discovered that the Hutterites and the Mennonites in the region had the same idea for their colonies, sending girls to college also. The four girls got along wonderfully and supported each other throughout their time there. 'The Four Musketeers' they'd called themselves. Since graduating she has become a veritable link between the Amish and the wider medical community which benefited both tremendously.

An hour later Veronica heard the horse and buggy returning. She raced to the door to meet them. She was beside herself. The nurse would know what to do. Surely it couldn't be that serious, Veronica kept telling herself, though she was unconvinced, overcome with worry, exhausted from her watch over their beloved child.

"Please tell us what to do. I'm sick with worry," Veronica told Phoebe.

"Well, I'll see what I can do," Phoebe said as she hung her coat and black travelling bonnet on one of the pegs by the door. She walked into the kitchen and scrubbed her hands in the sink there. Then grabbing her purse, she took out a stethoscope and walked into the bedroom.

"So, you're feeling poorly, eh?" Phoebe asked. Rose looked up at her, though she didn't say anything. "I'm going to listen to your chest here," Phoebe explained. "Would that be okay?"

Rose nodded once, weakly. Then looking up at Veronica and Henry who were standing at the foot of the bed, she said, "I'm *chust* listening for asthma or pneumonia, maybe croup," she told them as she placed the ear buds in her ears and listened to Rose's chest.

"Hm," Phoebe said. "Not sure it's one of those. When did you first notice she was sick?" she asked.

"A few hours ago. The coughing woke me," Veronica explained. "And she was burning up. She hadn't been too sharp yesterday evening, either. We sponged her and tried to get the fever down. Then we gave her some tea. It helped a bit. I am *chust* so worried."

"Hm," was all Phoebe replied. Just then Rose was wracked with another bout of coughing. Phoebe frowned as she listened to Rose.

"I'm a bit worried about meningitis," Phoebe commented to the parents. At that Veronica asked desperately, "but *kinner* can die from that, can't they?"

"I think we might want to take her into the hospital before it gets any worse. Is that okay with you?" Phoebe asked carefully skirting Veronica's question.

"I think you'll want to get a van to *kumm*," she suggested, turning her gaze to Henry. He nodded and said, "I'll call. Be right back," as he headed first to the bedroom to quickly dress, jumping into his barndoor trousers right over his pajamas, and then out to the phone box by the barn.

He was back in a matter of minutes and could assure them that a van was on the way. Phoebe and Veronica dressed Rose in a light nightgown and wrapped her in a blanket. Mrs. Dyck arrived within ten minutes, her usual bubbly self.

"Oh dear. Not too well, eh?" she asked. "Well, mine got sick at that age, worried me to death and then all of a sudden, they're up and running around and you're a basket case by then and all wore out. Your girlie will be just fine. You'll see," she said, trying to be optimistic and reassuring.

Henry carried Rose to the car and passed her to Veronica in the back seat. The coughing didn't let up the whole time they were driving. Finally, they arrived at the hospital and hurried into the emergency room. Instantly they were ushered into a small cubicle and surrounded by nurses. Phoebe explained what had transpired thus far, the nurses nodding and taking notes as she spoke. A doctor whom she recognized from her time in the hospital while shadowing the nurses during her training was there, also.

Phoebe passed on her observations. The doctor listened to Rose's chest and had her open her mouth and stick out her tongue. She was quite short of breath when she wasn't coughing.

"Frankly, I'm worried about meningitis," Phoebe told the doctor. He nodded ever so slightly. His grim visage becoming even more grim, were that possible.

"Let's get some tests going. And start an IV. She's probably dehydrated too. Keep her cool. I'll be back shortly," the doctor explained, and as an afterthought, whispered to the head nurse standing by the door, "immediate isolation protocol. If it is meningitis we won't know if it's viral or bacterial for a while till we hear back from the lab. Best to err on the side of caution. Also do a pertussis culture." When Phoebe overheard that her heart stopped. If she had been exposed to meningitis or Whooping Cough along with the family, she wouldn't be able to go home to her own husband and children without exposing them all to it, too. In a close-knit community like the Amish, it could spread like wildfire, especially since most did not immunize their children. Even after starting antibiotics, it could take three weeks of isolation to guarantee she won't contract it, too. If it turns out Rose does have meningitis, she'd be looking at a similar incubation period where, even after starting antibiotics, she could become a carrier and pass it on to others. Her thoughts went back to her twins. Then came the horrible thought: she knew she was 'in the family way,' but probably not even four weeks yet. Depending on the diagnosis this could also mean trouble. She tried not to imagine that, saying a silent prayer instead. And then another one.

As soon as the nurses were finished connecting Rose to all the monitors, oxygen, IV, and a pulse oximeter to check the level of her blood gases, they left the room. Rose slept on, the cough abating for now. The door was closed and the window in the door covered with a large sign alerting all that this was now designated an isolation site and all visitors were required to check in at the nurses' station before entering. A table was placed outside the room in the hall with masks, gowns, sterile gloves, shoe covers, hair nets and disposable stethoscopes among other medical paraphernalia. Yes, disposable! Each one meant to be thrown away after each exam, however brief. This was serious contamination control.

Finally left alone, Henry looked at Veronica and Phoebe and said one word.

"*Brau.*" At that all three fell to their knees next to the bed and silently prayed in earnest, storming heaven, for sure.

Keep an open mind, but don't keep it too open or people will throw a lot of rubbish into it.
~ From an Amish cookbook

CHAPTER 18

The Queen's Finger

It was indeed Whooping Cough in the end, and it was a long slog until Rose was better. Everything slowly returned to normal when she returned home. Phoebe hunkered down with the family for another ten days and then was able to return to her own family. Phoebe marveled at how many jigsaw puzzles one family could do in ten days, not to mention the games: Monopoly, Scrabble, Dutch Blitz, Cribbage and Happy Families—that old British card game, among others.

One of the little boys in their district who had gotten to know Rose at church on Sundays brought over one of a recent litter of his Holland lop-eared rabbits when he heard she was sick. He'd won ribbons for his pedigree rabbits at the county fairs. The rabbit could live indoors or out and keep her company while she recovered. After much discussion, the two children decided on naming it Honey Bunny. Clarence could visit Rose if they stayed out of doors, and he wore a mask. He was more than delighted to comply and sat in the sun in the yard with Rose and the bunny whom she would enjoy for many years to come. Henry recommended putting Honey Bunny with her little calf in the barn for company. Both animals seemed perfectly happy with the new arrangement. Rose could take Honey Bunny outdoors and sit in the sun on the grass in the yard with the rabbit in her lap for hours. Rose said Clarence looked like a doctor when he wore the mask and took to calling her little friend Dr. Zook. (His family name was Zook.)

Henry returned from the phone shack after breakfast the second day home after spending more than a week in the hospital. Rose was already in the barn cuddling and talking to the rabbit. After depositing his boots at the mud room mat, he washed his hands at the chore sink by the door. Sitting down at the table he removed his hat and reached for the mug of steaming coffee Veronica set before him.

"Well, turns out they had it, too," he announced.

"Oh, really?" Veronica was genuinely surprised. "I see. Are they alright now?"

"Ya, finally. A bunch of hospital visits but the last one in bed is getting better. They said they never thought it would end. Changes your life in an instant, eh?"

"I was so afraid of losing Rose," Veronica said, her eyes tearing up once again.

"We don't have enough faith, I figure," Henry said shaking his head.

"But would I have any faith left at all if we'd lost her? I *chust* don't know," Veronica fretted.

"Worry ends where faith begins," Henry reminded her.

"Sorry, but I'm *chust* not there. Not yet. Now I'm afraid all that sickness might have affected the baby somehow too. Measles can leave devastating side effects, ya know. Maybe Whooping Cough does too."

"Guess you should go see that midwife and ask her," Henry advised. "I am thinking *mamms chust* need something to worry about all the time, though. They wouldn't be *mamms* otherwise then would they, eh?" It was Henry's attempt at a joke. It was not appreciated.

"This isn't a laughing matter, Henry. I lost one *bobbel* too many already," she said as she wiped her eyes and then honked into her handkerchief, "and I can't believe *Gott* would make me go through all that again."

Henry got up and took Veronica in his arms. She melted into his chest.

"What would I do without you?" she asked.

"You wouldn't be having another *bobbel* for sure if you didn't have me, for one," he said chuckling. She blushed.

"Problem solved, then," he added. Just then they heard the pitter patter of little feet as Rose skipped into the kitchen.

"You two are always *shmuzzling*," she complained, coming into the kitchen.

"It's 'cause we love each other so much," Henry explained, chuckling.

"Stop, youse," Veronica whispered through gritted teeth, and poked him in the ribs for emphasis, stepping back a step from the embrace.

"What 'cha gonna do today?" Rose wanted to know.

Veronica spoke first. "Well, you and I, Missy, are going to finish up addressing the *Grischtdaag* cards and send those off. You get to stick all those stamps on."

"Aren't you lucky?" Henry said sarcastically.

"Then we'll start the peanut brittle," Veronica said, sending a steely glare at Henry. He acknowledged her reaction with a wink. She was too miffed to blush this time.

"That will be one of our gifts," Veronica explained, "and we'll plan out the rest. I've started a list so we can check each thing off as we make them. How does that suit her royal highness?"

Rose thought a moment. Then she observed, "You two are higher up than I am, so how can I be a 'highness'?"

Henry let out one of his delightful guffaws. "Out of the mouths of babes, eh?" he whispered to Veronica from behind his hand. She answered the question, pushing him back.

"Well, *liebling*, it's *chust* a figure of speech, like addressing a queen or something." That answer didn't quite explain anything at all, as far as Rose was concerned.

"'Dressing a queen's finger?" she asked, now completely baffled. "That's *ferhoodled* if you ask me."

"No one asked you," Henry corrected her, flummoxed by her forwardness.

"Never mind, Rose. I'll explain it later," Veronica said. "Here, take the rag on the sink. Why don't you wipe off the table and we can finish up those *Grischtdaag* cards. I really need you to help me now, Rose." *She's too schmart for her own gut,* Veronica mused to herself. *I'm thinking Henry and I will have to talk about this, how do you raise* kinner *to respect their elders without squashing their childlikeness and sense of wonder? I don't remember having one like this when I was teaching. Not in my whole time at that* schooss, *in all those years.*

For the next hour Veronica signed cards while Rose had a heyday affixing Christmas stickers to the brown paper cards they had made embellished with potato prints in green and red. All that was left after that was Rose's signature, which was surprisingly legible for a four-almost-five-year-old. She slowly, painstakingly wrote her name inside each one in pencil, while biting her tongue which was supposed to help in the process, somehow. When she was done, she slid the cards over to Veronica's side of the table for her to sign, too. Watching closely as Veronica wrote, Rose was horrified to see Veronica writing 'Henry' and under that 'and Veronica.'

"But *Dat* must sign his own name, *Mamm*. You can't sign it for him. He's gotta do it," she explained, blatantly scandalized.

"Well, for *Grischtdaag* cards, people often sign them that way for both..." she began.

"But that's not right," Rose cut in and demanded.

"Okay, we'll save these for later, then," Veronica said, then adding to herself, *while I figure out how to explain this one. Whew. Nothing's easy. I'd forgotten how legalistic kinner can be; there's only black and white to them, no in-between anything,* she thought to herself. *I might need to rethink that wish of mine to have twelve of 'em...But then it's Gott who sends them. And supposedly the grace too, then, along with each one. I'm thinking she's chust way to schmart for her own gut. And You gave her not one but TWO teachers for parents. You'd think we could figure out this one. Huh....*

"Okay, now," Veronica said taking stock of all they had accomplished that day. "Cards are in the mailbox to be picked up, peanut brittle is cooling on the granite slab, dinner is *chust* about ready. Then we can make those snowflakes for when we visit Eli and Hazel, eh?" she asked Rose who was standing at the sink on her little wooden stool, licking off the last of the sticky goo on the spoon they'd used to scrape out the last drops of peanut brittle from the kettle. Rose offered one nod in affirmation as she continued licking that thick lovely golden coat of sticky stuff on the spoon. The pots were soaking in the sink. Veronica would tackle those later.

"When you are finished with the spoon, let's leave the pots for now and you can set the table. *Dat* will be here soon. I'll start putting the food out," Veronica instructed

Rose. Finally, when she could no longer taste any peanut brittle on the spoon, convinced she'd licked it clean, she dropped it into the sink and began setting the table for the noon meal. Henry walked into the mud room shortly after that, kicking off his mud boots and went to wash up.

"Sure smells *gut* in here. Peanut brittle, too?" He asked.

"Ya," Rose answered. "And we're gonna make *kaffi* paper snowflakes for Hazel and Eli this afternoon. We're gonna visit them soon," she informed him.

"We got another *mamm* sheep out there who I figure will have her lamb tonight if I'm right," he said as he came to the table.

"Can I name it? Please?" Rose asked as she scooted onto the bench at the long table.

"Let's see if it's a boy or a girl first, eh? Ya don't want to name a boy Daisy or Matilda, I'm guessing," *Dat* said, laughing.

"Oh, you're right," Rose agreed, soberly reflecting on that piece of advice.

"*Patties down?*" Henry asked, to signal the silent grace for the meal. After a full two minutes he asked, "What's in this bowl?"

Rose jumped in before Veronica could inform him of the menu that day. "That one is ham pie, and that one is corn salad," she stood up at her place, pointing out each one.

"I got to cut up the peppers and celery. I'm gonna be a *gut* cook when I growed up and get a *halsband*," she explained to Henry quite matter of fact, and quickly went on.

"And those are Southern Gal Biscuits. *Mamm* made those," she explained, sitting back down.

"So, you had that little chat then already?" he asked Veronica in English, surprised the matter had already been dealt with so quickly. Then the little chatterbox slathered some Sweet Amish Peanut Butter Spread onto a biscuit and took a giant bite. Veronica grabbed the moment to talk to Henry. This would definitely be an English-only adult discussion.

"I made an appointment with Midwife Ruth for tomorrow morning."

"*Gut* idea," Henry agreed as he reached for another biscuit.

"Well, I was hoping you'd watch Rose here while I'm gone. I hope to talk to Ruth about some of my concerns, the recent bout of Whooping Cough being one of them."

"Oh, sure. We'll be *chust* fine." Switching back to Pennsylvania Dutch he inquired, "When do you want to leave?"

"Before nine maybe, if you can time take off, that is," she asked.

"Yup, that'll be fine," he answered before taking another generous slice of the ham pie.

"And maybe bring home some ice cream?" Henry asked. Rose perked up and said excitedly, "When? Today?"

Henry answered. "No tomorrow. I've got plenty to do here, wanna help me?" he asked. Rose vigorously nodded in agreement.

Use it up, wear it out, make it do, or do without.
- Plain Saying

CHAPTER 19

Fly Paper

"Pertussis during pregnancy is not dangerous for the mother or infant unless the mother is still infectious when the baby is born," Midwife Ruth explained. "If you don't have symptoms when you are at nine months you don't have to worry. You're so close to nine now, and you don't have any symptoms, so we don't have to even consider it. I promise."

"Whew. I sure was nervous about that. Gosh. So, everything is looking *gut* then?" Veronica asked, genuinely relieved. The earth sure was full of dangerous germs. How could she avoid them all? How could she *not* worry.

"His heart sounds strong and you are gaining *chust* right," Ruth said.

"It's not too small? My last one stopped growing even before I was this far along," Veronica explained, not yet believing things could be normal after all the complications with her first and last pregnancy.

"No, I'd say he is way up there for weight so far. Your blood pressure is great, you aren't at all anemic or showing any proteins in your urine. I'd say you are really in tip-top shape," Ruth assured her, adding, "textbook perfect, actually."

"I don't want any of those ultrasounds or amnio-sen... sen...whatever tests this time. I'd *chust* freak out if anything said there was a problem," Veronica said, wiping her eyes and then her nose with her handkerchief. Just then she burst into sobs, unable to contain her fear any longer. Ruth put her arm around Veronica's shoulders.

"There, there. It's natural to worry during pregnancy but you've got more than most after all you went through the first time. But I guarantee you are really fine, and your baby is really doing well, too."

"I can't help it..." Veronica sniffed, trying to regain her composure.

"I understand," Ruth said. "You can start thinking about where you want to give birth. You can have this one at home or in the hospital, the birthing suites there are really nice. Let me know what you think. We've got time to decide."

"Really?" Veronica blinked and tucked the handkerchief away. This for sure was different from the last time. That had been a nightmare from which she felt she'd never wake up.

She drove herself home in the buggy to find Henry and Rose hard at work in the kitchen. Rose heard the horse clip-clopping up the driveway first and ran out to meet her *Mamm* at the kitchen door.

"*Mamm! Mammmmm!* We're makin' fly paper. *Dat* says the old stuff is *yunge,* so we're cooking the new ones. A small farmer gave him the recipe. *Dat* showed me. You cook some oil, like lard or lamp oil, he said, but we've got that nice coconut oil, so we used that. And melt resin—I thought at first, he wanted raisins—and then we take it off the stove and cool it until it looks like honey, not too runny or too thick. I tasted it. It's yummy but *Dat* says it's for the flies, not me," at which Veronica gasped and glared at Henry who only shrugged, as if he could have prevented her from tasting it.

Rose continued. "He says I can eat fluffy peanut butter or Traffic Jam, but the flies get this stuff cause they can't have peanut butter or jam. Then we take a big paint brush and unroll some brown paper and sort of paint the goo on it and hang up the strips from the beams when it's dry."

"That is great. I didn't think I was going to get to that anytime soon. Thanks, you two," Veronica said as Henry went out to stable the horse.

Back in the house Henry looked at Veronica while Rose puttered around the kitchen helping to put their project away. The strips of fly paper were carefully laid in the dry sink on top of newspaper to dry overnight. Every few minutes Rose would skip across the kitchen and stand on her toes to look over the edge of the sink and check on it. Veronica looked back and smiled and nodded, conveying the message to Henry that all was well from her trip to the midwife. Henry relaxed then and smiled back. Then he winked at her. That always got her blushing. She couldn't help it.

"*Dat*, is that *Small Farmers' Journal* thing made by small farmers? Ya know, Little People like *Onkel* Orla?" Rose asked him. Henry looked at Veronica then and they both broke out laughing. Finally, Henry tried to answer.

"Well, I don't know, but I am guessing not. That is it *chust* means they have a small farm, not too big."

"Oh," Rose answered, satisfied with that answer. "But why is *Onkel* Orla so little?"

Veronica tried to explain. "Sometimes people are born different from other people. *Gott* makes us all different, all unique in a way. We think that special people, those born with things like Downs, like Poppy has, or *Onkel* Orla has something called dwarfism, well, it gives the rest of us a very big opportunity to show extra love to *Gott's* special children. He decides which *kinner* will be born into which families and knows they will be the perfect parents and brothers and sisters for that child." That closed the topic for Rose. Her next question was far more pressing.

"Did ya bring home ice cream *Mamm?*" she wanted to know. Veronica nodded her head.

"So, y'all leave room for ice cream, right?" Rose exclaimed and continued before awaiting an answer.

"Did you know *Mamm,* that *Dat* is making a Scrabble game for Edith and Milo's family for *Grischtdaag?* I got to sand some of the little tiles. Did you know there are fifty-two of them in one game? I can count to fifty-two." Then she revised her answer.

"Well, almost. *Dat* helped me. *Mamm,* did ya know there are twelve 'e's in a Scrabble set, and did ya know there are only one X and one J? It will take a lot of time, but he says their old set should have been burned long ago. Did he tell you what else we wanna make for their gifts?" Their little chatter box was charged up now.

"...and a marble shoot where the marbles fall down tracks in a maze that is standing up? And a checkers set, and hockey sticks for the boys, but he says we'll buy some of the presents for them, like a new Monopoly game and a baseball glove, and he's making a Button String Whirligig, too...."

"No, my love. I didn't know that. You've been busy, huh?" Veronica asked. The tears were coming back once more. She thought to herself, *so now how did I get so lucky?*

Well, not luck. Blessed. You've blessed me beyond my wildest dreams. 'For it shall be given unto you; good measure, pressed down, shaken together, and running over.' *Blessing after blessing. First Henry, then Rose, and now a new bobbel kumming. *How could I have ever doubted that You love me? That I am so very, very loved? Oh, ye of little faith. It's such a miracle I have faith at all. Even that is a gift. I for sure would be in bad shape if it were not for that.*

*Luke 6:38

Swallowing pride rarely gives you indigestion.
~ From an Amish cookbook

CHAPTER 20
Joyeux Noël

I
t was raining. Pouring down actually. Rose stood staring out the living room window.

"*Dat* said it's 'raining cats and dogs,' *Mamm*. What does that mean?" she called from her sentinel.

Veronica answered from the kitchen doorway. "*Chust* one of those funny expressions. That would be quite amazing if dogs and cats were falling from the sky, eh?"

"Oh. Like when *Dat* told me to keep your *Grischtdaag* present a secret, he said I shouldn't 'let the cat out of the bag?' I can't tell you, ya know. We don't even have a cat in the house. They all live in the barn, for the mice mainly," she reasoned. Veronica chuckled to herself. What would Rose think up next? Veronica didn't have to wait long for the answer to that question.

"*Mamm*, can you spell 'mouse trap' with only three letters?" she quizzed Veronica.

"*Dat* told me this one, *Mamm*." Veronica shook her head, unable to come up with a solution.

"I give up," she said.

Rose answered: "C-A-T" and burst out laughing. Veronica groaned, shaking her head.

"*Gut* one," she agreed.

"The farmers need the rain, Rose. They've been praying for it for weeks. The crops won't finish growing without it. Even the last of our kitchen garden will perk up after this. You'll see," Veronica told her as Rose slowly walked to the window once more. Then Veronica heard a tiny voice singing mournfully from the next room: "Rain, rain go away...little Rosie wants to play...rain, rain go away...come again another day...."

"Hey, Rose," Veronica called. "Want to help me put out second breakfast?"

"Okay," a very dejected child answered and dragged her feet to the kitchen. Just then a brighter thought occurred to her. "*Mamm*, what are we gonna do for *Grischtdaag* today?"

"Well, we've finished the snowflakes, and the paper chains are ready for over the windows and doors, and the peanut brittle is done...." Veronica recalled the list they'd made.

"*Dat* is picking up some pretty candles in town later, and I found the box of red ribbons... oh, and he promised to get some Balsam boughs for us to decorate the windowsills with."

"We haven't made the clothes pin family for the little ones yet, ya know, Lenny, Louie, and Ruby. And you said we'd bring 'em a moss garden, too. But we can't get the moss today I'm guessing," she said and then added with a sly smile, "because it's raining cats and dogs, like."

Veronica was rummaging around in one of the bottom

cupboards in the kitchen as they talked. "I found it!" she exclaimed.

"What?" Rose asked.

"Here's an old pie tin you can use for the moss garden. Set it on the floor in the mud room to remind us tomorrow, okay?" Rose did as she was told.

"Why don't you set the table next. I'm *chust* stirring the sausage gravy. *Kaffi* is done and the waffles are all made. Your *dat* will be here any minute for second breakfast," Veronica told Rose.

"You never said yes, though. Can we paint the clothespin people today?" Rose asked again.

"Very *gut* idea. You can start by pushing them into their little stands. I've already cut down the height for the *mamms* and the *kinner*," Veronica explained.

"Oh, look!" Rose pointed to the ceiling. "*Dat* already put the fly paper up."

"And there are already flies on it since last night," Veronica noted.

"*Dat* told me that on Sunday we can finish the Scrabble game. He needs to write the letters out and spray it all, he said."

"And I want to make you a new dress for *Grischtdaag* and when we visit Canada," Veronica said.

"And will you make one to match for Rosemary too?" Rose asked.

"Did she say she wanted one?" Veronica asked, playing along.

"I'll have to go ask her," Rose said as she headed for the stairs.

As Rose took leave, Veronica remembered the quote from the little calendar on her dresser that she checked in with every morning.

*With God, everything has its place. The immense tranquility of
God's order should be found in every room. - C.D.*

Plenty of food for thought, she mused.

When Rose came back downstairs Henry had just
walked into the kitchen for breakfast, having first kicked off
his barn boots in the mud room.

"We must have forgotten about the mail yesterday," he
said, dropping a rather large bundle of letters on the table
on his way to the sink.

"Oh, goodie!" Rose yelled as she came into the kitchen.
"Are there *Grischtdaag* cards? Ya think?" she asked excitedly.

"There's a *gut* chance there are," he replied.

"Who are they all from?" she wanted to know.

"Well, let's see," Henry said as he sat down at the table
and slit the first envelope open with his pocketknife.

"It says Eli and Hazel. And she painted one of her
winter watercolor scenes on it," he said, admiring it.

"Oh, how sweet," Veronica said as she brought the gravy
to the table. "Let's eat and then we can open them all."

"And then we'll hang them up?" Rose asked. Both
Veronica and Henry nodded.

"*Patties down?*" Henry asked.

After the silent prayer he ladled rich sausage gravy over
his waffles. Then he nodded to Rose, in answer to her question about hanging up the Christmas cards, his mouth
already full of waffles and gravy.

After a few bites Rose remembered her doll, Rosemary.

"*Mamm,* Rosemary says she wants a new *gaund* for
Grischtdaag, too."

"Okay. Maybe you can help me sew it, too," Veronica
said.

Then a thought occurred to Veronica. "Maybe we should

brush up on our French. We'll be in Milverton in three weeks.

"*Joyeux noël*," Henry jumped into the discussion. "*Bonne idée.*"

"*Même moi, je comprends cela,*" Veronica said, laughing.

"*Pennsylfaani* pleeeeeease," Rose whined.

"Well, they say it's a whole lot easier to learn a new language when they're little," Henry said. "No excuse we can't try now," he reasoned, in English.

"Even I understood you," Veronica added, chuckling.

"*Pennsylfaani* pleeeeeease," Rose repeated her request, louder this time, while stamping a small foot for emphasis.

Sorry we can't come to the door just now. Please leave a message.
Do not wait for the beep. There is none.
- Sign on the door of an Amish shop.

CHAPTER 21

Husband's Delight

"Do they know we're *kumming?*" Rose asked Henry the next day.

"Who are you talking about?" her *Dat* asked from behind the newspaper he was reading in his bentwood hickory rocker.

"*Onkel* Milo and *Aendi* Edith and all," Rose explained. "Do they know?"

"I don't know if they told the *kinner* or if they're keeping it a surprise. I'll ask next time I call," he assured her.

"When will *Mamm* get home?" Rose moped by his chair.

"Pretty soon," he replied.

"Why does she keep having to see her friend Ruth?" Rose asked.

"Well, uh," Henry hedged. "I guess they're *gut* friends, that's why."

"Humph," Rose groused. "Mary is my *friede,* and I don't see *her* every week."

"Well, I guess Ruth is giving her some more of those vitamins," he could tell her honestly.

"Oh. *Mamm* said we can start baking *Grischtdaag* cookies

when she gets home. *Mamm* said we can make gingerbread first. We might even make a gingerbread house, *Dat*."

"They're called Braxton-Hicks contractions. Some say they are just practice contractions. They don't last. They're perfectly normal," Midwife Ruth tried to convince Veronica that nothing was wrong, and she need not worry.

"But you're sure I'm not going into labor too early? How will you know?" Veronica fretted. "I mean, this feels like what happened last time," Veronica asked as she twisted the handkerchief in her lap into knots.

"Your baby is growing well. His heart sounds perfect. Nothing at all points to *anything* that's a concern. It's normal to be worried when you're expecting, and you have all the past trauma besides. We *chust* must get you to nine months. Anything after thirty-five weeks is safe. Forty weeks is ideal. So far there is absolutely nothing that tells me you have anything to worry about," Ruth tried to reassure Veronica once again.

Then Veronica asked, "By the way, has that other midwife, Anna, found anyone to replace me as her apprentice? Any interesting births?"

"Not really," Ruth said. "The clinic signed on two more students, both nurses who any of the midwives can call for backup if none of the other midwives are free. That's been a great help. And we had one baby born in the caul recently, where the bag of water hasn't broken, and the baby is born still in it. Quite amazing. Only about one in eighty-thousand births is like that and I got to see it!"

Back in the buggy on the way home Veronica prayed. *Help me to stop worrying. You've given me a whole new baby, and Rose, and Henry, besides. So many blessings, and all I do is fret. I need to relax and enjoy Your blessings, be grateful.* Just then the baby kicked. And kicked again. Veronica laughed as she rubbed her growing belly. "What are ya telling me, eh?" she spoke aloud. "You agree I worry too much, or you agree you are *chust* fine? Maybe both?" She laughed again as the baby continued to kick.

"Well, ya, I know you're there. You can stop kicking me now," she said, still laughing. "You can hear me, can't ya? But you don't have a clue what I'm saying, I bet." Shaking her head she recalled the quote from the little inspirational calendar on her dresser. This morning's offering had touched her profoundly. She'd go on to ponder it several more times that day.

Let this Christmas be for us a turning point. Let us become small enough to kneel at the crib and big enough just to reach the level of the Baby's eyes. Let us look into them and catch sight of Love Incarnate! Then we shall be made whole again, and our hunger will be filled. - C.D.

"*Mamm...Maaaammmm!*" Rose yelled as she came running from the house when she heard the buggy crunching up the driveway, careful to stay on the grass as she'd been instructed numerous times.

"*Dat* and I made dinner! And we finished the Scrabble game for *Onkel's Grischtdaag* gift. And you said we could make the cookies today, too," the little chatterbox rattled on, following the buggy into the barn. Henry came into the barn then and took over the task of taking the horse out of the harness shafts and leading him out to the paddock.

"What did you make for dinner?" Veronica asked.

"Oh, that *Halsband's* Delight Casserole. It was easy. And I got to set the table and get the *bredder* and the butter and pickled beets from down the cellar," Rose explained, feeling very grown up.

"Of course it was easy," Henry laughed. "Your *Mamm* made it before she left. All we had to do was fire up the oven and stick it in."

"But I *did* get to make it. Before *Mamm* left. She let me stir the meat on the stove and then I dumped the noodles in the water. She had everything in cups. I dumped in the cream cheese, sour cream and garlic, and...um...oh, and the salt. Then you stir it all up and dump it in a glass thingy. Then you dump tomato sauce on top and then all the cheese bits. See? I am learning how to cook, *Dat,* and I got to set the table and...." Rose turned back to Veronica and prattled on.

"So, is everything *gut?*" Henry whispered to Veronica at the sink where they were both washing up.

Rose continued informing them of all the things she had stored up to tell her mother.

"And someday I'll cook for a *halsband* and all my *kinner,* too." She paused, frowned, and address them once more, "Say, where do all the *kinner kumm* from anyway?" she wanted to know.

Her parents looked at one another. Veronica chose to answer this one...or not.

"Well, let go see about this yummy dinner, eh?" she asked.

"Ya. I *chust* worry too much," she told Henry, switching back to English, bringing up the midwife visit again.

"It's all *gut.*"

Henry bumped shoulders with her then. "See. Worry ends where faith begins," he quoted the old Amish adage as he dried his hands. Before leaving the sink, he put one arm around her shoulders and pulled her into a proper hug. She stiffened and whispered, "Not here!"

Letting go he sighed, resigned to letting that embrace go for now and asked, "So it's cookies this afternoon then?" Of course, Rose answered the question.

"Ya. Gingerbread first. After dinner. You can take it out of the oven now, *Dat*," Rose said.

"Oh. So now I have your permission then?" he said looking over at Veronica. They both shook their heads. Then Veronica whispered, switching back to English as she passed him once more on her way to the table, "what'll she be like when she's twelve? Or sixteen?" she asked in a low voice as she threw a hot pad on the table for Henry to set the hotdish on.

"I know," he answered grimly. "But honey, by then there'll be two of them, maybe more...." He could not contemplate such a thing.

"We might have two by Second Christmas *this* year, never mind when she's twelve," Veronica whispered, rolling her eyes.

One of the most complicated tasks modern man faces today is trying to figure out how to live a simple life.
- Amish saying

CHAPTER 22

Brother Heinrich's Christmas

Veronica wrapped her long tresses in a dry towel, her bath towel already hanging up on the wall-mounted wooden spider between the wood stove and the ancient clawfoot tub in the basement. She'd bathed in it as far back as she could remember. Most likely so had her own *mamm* and even *Grossmammi* when she was little.

Rose had bathed earlier, and Henry would reuse the water for the last time before he tucked in for the night, adding a bit of hot water from the canning kettle on the old stove in the cellar and then unplugging the tub drain when he was done, sending the water out into the orchard. Before heading for the stairs Veronica took two more logs from the pile near the door and chucked them into the old Erie wood stove. The *kesselhaus* would stay toasty warm for the next person and the heat would steadily rise, wafting through the wrought iron grate in the ceiling of the *kesselhaus* and then the grate in the floor of the loft above that, and warm the house for the night.

Veronica slowly climbed the stairs, huffing and puffing

all the way up from the basement *kesselhaus* and met Henry in the kitchen where he'd been reading *The Budget* at the table while he waited for his turn at the tub.

"This is a *gut* one," he began. "Listen to this," he prefaced as he hunted for what he was looking for. "Here it is," he finally announced. "It says here that 'some people eat only from the three basic food groups: canned, frozen and take-out.' Someone from Pinecraft sent it in," he chuckled.

Folding the paper and laying it on the table, he stood up and walked to her. He held her in his arms for a long time. She smelled so lovely. He could stand here like this forever and he would be happy.

"I love you," he whispered softly as they pulled apart.

"Your little *meedel* is wide awake and waiting for a bedtime story from her *mamm*," he informed her.

"I still don't believe she is really ours sometimes, ya know?" Veronica whispered.

"Well, ya better believe it and there'll be another one *kumm* sometime after *Grishtadaag*," he grinned.

Then more soberly he added, "*Chust* don't idolize her. Ya know, at the expense of leaving off teaching what is right and wrong and not disciplining them." She nodded. *Yes, some do that to their children,* she admitted to herself.

Then she brought up, once more, her doubts about the trip.

"Do you still think it's safe to travel for Second Christmas? All the way to Milverton? I mean it would be early, I'm not exactly due until mid-January, or later, according to the midwife, so we should be back home, right?" she worried.

"Then we should be *gut*. You worry too much, my *frau*," he said, moving in for another hug.

"You go bathe now," she said, deciding to avoid another hug. The fact was that he smelled more like the barn than the *halsband* she normally could hardly wait to hug, at bedtime.

"I'll go get the story started," she said turning toward the stairs, taking a deep breath once more before facing the steep steps before her.

"Brother Heinrich's Christmas," Veronica began reading the new book after settling herself next to Rose on their bed, the book propped up on her chest.

"This fable, or legend, tells us that a very long time ago, hundreds of years ago* in a great stone monastery covered with ivy and grape vines, lived a monk called Brother Heinrich. Now the monks were men who loved the Lord very much and had dedicated their lives to prayer and helping other people to love *Gott,* too. The monks in this monastery where they all lived made wine to sell. It was known as the best wine in all the land. Brother Heinrich's job was to lead his donkey in a big circle all day, every day, pulling the long handle of the wine press round and round to press the grapes."

"Sort of like our cider press?" Rose interjected.

"Yes, exactly like that," Veronica confirmed before she went on.

"It was very boring work, but each one living there had to do their job. So, Brother Heinrich talked to his donkey while they trudged around the press all day. His donkey was named Sigismund.

"Now Brother Heinrich loved to sing and the Abbot— the head of the monastery—made Brother Heinrich in charge of the choir. The trouble was that Sigismund also liked to sing and Brother Heinrich would sneak Sigismund into the back of the church choir whenever they practiced. Sigismund only knew two notes, though. 'Hee and Haw.' But no one minded. It was *chust* Sigismund.

"Then one day, one of the other brothers came running out to the wine press, all out of breath. He said to Brother Heinrich, 'Hurry, the Abbot wants to see you in his office right away. Hurry.' Bother Heinrich thought to himself, *Oh dear. I must be in some kind o' trouble,* and he went to see the Abbot.

"'I *chust* got a letter today from the Archbishop, Brother Abbot said." Veronica stopped then to explain.

"The Archbishop is sort of like the high mucky-muck elder in their church and only came to see the brothers once a year," she told Rose who nodded that she understood now.

"'So, he is coming for our Christmas day church service and our Christmas dinner afterwards,' he told Brother Heinrich. Now we must clean the monastery from top to bottom and polish all the floors and mend all the habits for such a special visit.'" As an aside Veronica informed Rose that 'habits' were what the monks' coarse homespun robes were called.

"'So, I have summoned you to have you practice the best songs with the choir for his visit. Now go and get to work!' the Abbot ordered him. And then he added, 'and you keep that ridiculous animal out of choir. What would the Archbishop think?' he asked, shaking his head in disgust."

"So, they practiced, and they practiced, but the brothers all grumbled. 'We sing these every year. They are so old and boring,' they complained. The Abbot thought so too when he came to see how they were doing at choir. Then he ordered Brother Heinrich to write a *new* Christmas hymn especially for the Archbishop's visit. Now this really made

Brother Heinrich nervous, but being an obedient monk, he wrote and wrote with his quill pen and parchment paper, trying to compose a new Christmas song, but nothing really *gut* came out of all his hard work. 'What are we to do, Sigismund?' he desperately asked the donkey on their way back to the barn that night. 'I *chust* can't write it.'

"And Sigismund replied mournfully, 'hee-haw.' Brother Heinrich dragged his feet as they went on toward the barn, that is until he suddenly stopped. 'What is that?' he asked. 'Listen.' He said, turning toward Sigismund. It *chust* kept getting louder and louder, and the sky kept getting brighter and brighter, and when they both looked up, they saw the sky was filled with angels all singing the most beautiful hymn they'd ever heard. The angels sang on and on, but then, all of a sudden, they were gone, and the sky was dark again. Brother Heinrich and Sigismund had fallen on the ground when they first saw the angels and looked at each other in utter bewilderment. 'Did the angels really sing that Sigismund? We must go back and write it all down. I think it is our new Christmas song,' he said in utter amazement as they turned around and ran back to his little room. He lit a candle and wrote out all the words with his quill pen on parchment paper and then the music too, thanking *Gott* for sending the angels with the song. When he got to the end, however, he couldn't remember exactly how it went. He tried to write different endings but none of them really worked. Brother Heinrich hummed the song he had written and stopped near the end, worried that the ending as the angels sang it was now lost forever. Suddenly Sigismund let out one of his giant hee-haws. Those two notes. That was it! They were the last stanza of the song. Quickly Brother Heinrich wrote in the ending as Sigismund had *chust* sung it. It was perfect.

"So, he brought the new song to the monks early the next morning and they practiced and practiced. They all marveled at the story Brother Heinrich told them and they said they'd never heard a more beautiful song before.

"And then the great day arrived, and they were all in the church ready for the service to begin. The brothers told Brother Heinrich that he *had* to bring Sigismund to the choir because he was the one that remembered the ending. The Abbot didn't see him at first but became furious when he noticed the donkey at the back of the choir stalls, but then it was too late to do anything about him.

"The service went beautifully, and the Archbishop marveled at the song. At the special Christmas dinner afterwards, the Archbishop told the monks that it was the most beautiful hymn he had ever heard, and that the dinner was positively the best Christmas dinner he had ever had, too. And then, looking down into his wine glass—he had already had several glasses which he also pronounced was the best wine in all the land—he told them that he had actually seen more astonishing things in his lifetime than a singing donkey in a choir stall and gave Sigismund his blessing."

Then Veronica explained, "It really is a real Christmas song, too. It was written in the 1600s in Latin originally, which is what the monks spoke, I guess. But here they have the words in the book, too." she said.

In dulci jubi lo
Let us our homage shew:
Our heart's joy reclineth
In praesepio;
And like a bright star shineth
Matris in gremio,
Alpha es et O!

O Jesu parvule,
My heart is sore for Thee!
Hear me, I beseech Thee,
O puer optime;
My praying let it reach Thee,
O princeps gloriae.
Trahe me post te.
O patris caritas!
O Nati lenitas!
Deeply were we stained.
Per nostra crimina:
But Thou for us hast gained
Coelorum gaudia,
Qualis gloria!
Ubi sunt gaudia,
If that they be not there?
There are Angels singing
Nova cantica;
And there the bells are ringing
In Regis curia.
O that we were there!

The lyrics are about Heinrich Suso, a 14th-century Dominican abbot, who according to legend, notated the carol In Dulci Jubilo after it had been sung to him by a band of angels; he was unexpectedly aided to finish it by Sigismund, his donkey.

He who sings prays twice.
~ Augustine of Hippo

CHAPTER 23

Hallicher Bebottsdaag!

T he first thing Veronica did when she got up each day was brush out her long hairs as she read her small calendar's offering for the day that sat on her dresser. It often surprised her how appropriate each little lesson could be, as if they were written just for her. Today's message was no different.

Christ desires to be born in the mangers of our hearts. Are the doors of our hearts wide open to receive the shepherds, the Magi, the stray visitors, in a word, humanity? Are they open to receive one another as Christ would receive each one of us? Are they open to receive those around us in our daily life? - C.D.

The calendar is a compilation of quotes written by a lay woman named Catherine Doherty, a contemporary and close friend of Dorthy Day who founded the Madonna House communities in Canada in the 1940s. She had lived and breathed service to those around her, especially the poor.

Henry came in from the barn for breakfast.

"We forgot about the mail again yesterday. Rose, it's your job now to remind us every day to check the mail," he said tossing a rather large bundle of it on the table. She nodded at once that she understood.

"Are there any *Grischtdaag* cards?" Veronica wanted to know.

"There's a lot of things, I'm guessing," he replied. "We'll open them at *mariye-esse,*" he said heading toward the sink to wash.

"So, what have you made for my breakfast then Rose?" he asked.

"My favorite, baked oatmeal," she giggled as she finished setting the places.

Veronica came slowly to the table carrying two coffee mugs, trying to catch her breath. She was for certain getting tired of being so tired, so very pregnant.

"Well, let's see here," he said as he sat down and announced grace.

"*Patties down?*" he asked. Then after a long minute as he cleared his throat, Rose immediately jumped in.

"*Dat,* did you know it's my *bebottsdaag* in four days? And I will be five? And I will be old enough to go to school in the fall? And I am already old enough to watch the *bobbeli* at the quilting, and I get to say what I want for dinner in four days."

"I see. Really? Is that so?" Henry asked while raising the mug to his lips, his eyebrows questioning this new...whatever it was, convention maybe?

"Did your *Mamm* tell you that?" he queried suspiciously as his eyes found Veronica's observing this exchange. She winked back at him, confirming Rose's allegation.

"Well, um, I guess congratulations are in order then. *Hallicher Bebottsdaag!*" her father pronounced.

"Oh, yes. Everyone does that. Gets to pick supper. I read it in *The Budget*. But I haven't decided yet, though. What I want. I think either Yummasetti or maybe McDonalds. Remember when we had that on our trip back from Milverton? What would you pick for your birthday *zapper* huh?"

But before he could answer he backed up a few seconds to be sure he heard what he thought he had heard. *You read it in The Budget, eh? Is that so? So, you can read now too?* he thought to himself. *Miracles never cease,* he chuckled before he answered.

"Hmmm. Well now, I reckon I'd have poutine. We had it on that same trip, remember. I am guessing your *mamm* will figure out how to make that, ya think?" he asked. Rose nodded.

"I think it's piping hot gravy over French fries with melty cheese curds topping it off. It's really *gut,* eh?" Veronica asked. Henry and Rose nodded in unison, their mouths full of oatmeal.

"Do you think I'll have a cake too? Maybe?" Rose pushed on.

"You *chust* stop asking, Missy. It's supposed to be a surprise, ya know," Veronica said. "Eat your oatmeal," Henry ordered, ending the discussion.

While Veronica began planning for the trip to Milverton in Ontario, Canada where Henry's brother Milo lived, Henry was at the carpentry bench in the barn finishing off the gifts for Milo's children for Second Christmas. Later in the day the three would take the buggy to Eli and Hazel's farm for dinner. Sarabeth insisted they come as the old people didn't get out so much anymore. She had become quite an accomplished cook and baker during her first year with them. For the two years before that, when she first left home, it was to be a *maud* for Faith after the terrible train and buggy accident that had claimed the lives of two of her children and Faith's husband. The women in the Amish community had made sure that Faith was never alone with her little baby Patience, who had been home with her while her husband, Noah, went to do errands in town with the two older children, Hope and Charity.

Christmas is less than two weeks away now. They would celebrate Christmas here with friends and family and, 'if hell don't freeze over and the creek don't rise'—one of Henry's pet sayings—they would travel to his hometown of Milverton, Ontario for *Ztvett Grischtdaag* and then back home again afterwards in plenty of time for the birth.

Rose was a veritable shadow, following Veronica everywhere, up and down the stairs, and of course, talking the entire time.

"Do you think they still don't know we're *kumming?*" she asked Veronica's backside as she chased her *mamm* up the stairs once again. When Veronica got to the top landing and stopped to catch her breath she answered, her arms full of folded laundry.

"No, I don't think they know. Milo told your *dat* when he called to check in with him yesterday that they've managed to keep it under wraps so far," Veronica explained as she wondered why children are blessed with so much more energy than their parents. *Very unfair,* she thought to herself while catching her breath, and hanging on to the banister. *Well, I shouldn't complain. What's wrong with me, anyway? All my fears and now I can tell this bobbel is definitely bigger than my last one. Maybe there's two? Heavens no! The midwife would have known by now. But Denki Gott! I should be happy to be schwanger forever if it meant healthy bobbeli. I guess I'll get to breathe again when it kumms, eh?*

"Do we need to make more peanut brittle? Or granola? Maybe we didn't make enough Christmas cookies for all of 'em. They are a lot of people, ya know," Rose pointed out.

Veronica nodded and headed back down to the kitchen.

"What I do know," Veronica said, "is that we're butchering Bacon tomorrow. It's finally cold enough and we don't want to put it off till the New Year," she told Rose, and then to herself, *and with a new* bobbel *by then, I won't be able to help at all.*

"Do we have to kill Bacon? He is such a nice pig," Rose said as she became still.

"We always butcher before *Grischtdaag*. We need the meat for the *kumming* year. That's why we live on a farm. We produce as much food as we can and work to have enough money to live this way, besides. And we pray for *gut* weather to grow everything and try to be *gut* stewards over all we've been given," Veronica tried to convey it without sounding too cold or callous. But those were the facts, given their way of life. The cycle would continue as long as there were farms and farmers and people needed to eat.

In order to enter Heaven, we must be lovers. For instance, we wash the dishes for love of God; we serve our family quietly and efficiently. When we connect serving with prayer, we grow in wisdom and love and become a light shining in the darkness of the world. This light of our loving service will lead people to God. ~ C.D.

CHAPTER 24

Everything But the Oink

The pig had been butchered a few days before. They would have fresh meat for Christmas. Waiting for cold weather toward the end of November usually ensured that the meat could be hung and 'aged' a bit without turning rancid. Without electricity this could be challenging. The various tasks associated with butchering had to be carefully planned. There were close to a hundred things you could do to process that much meat.

One periodical put it this way: "The Amish like to ham it up, literally. Most Amish households raise and butcher their own pigs which transform into a ready supply of bacon, hams, chops, ground pork, lard, puddings, pies and other dishes. Everything but the oink."

Lard, also called tallow, is the fat from pigs' abdomens. It can be rendered by trimming it from all the organs and cooking it slowly on a very low heat—93-113 degrees Fahrenheit—until it liquifies. It can then be strained and poured into canning jars and processed in a pressure canner and will keep all year. It will be a clear yellowish gold color, or white, depending on its purity. Leaf lard is the fat that surrounds the kidneys, and it is the very best lard for baking. When rendered, leaf lard is the most mild-flavored lard and will add flakiness to all your baked goods; think melt-in-your-mouth homemade pie crust and light fluffy biscuits.

Blood pudding and black pudding are the same dish, also known as blood sausage. It's a dark sausage that originated in the United Kingdom as a way to preserve meat and use animal blood that would otherwise go to waste. Rich in protein, black pudding is often made with pork blood, but can also be made with beef blood, and typically includes the following ingredients: oatmeal, barley flour or buckwheat flour, onions, and herbs and spices. It is often pressed into natural casings such as animal intestines, after they've been scrubbed clean.

Bone broth is a much-valued soup stock come winter. After cooking, the bones are reserved for making bone meal. Bone meal is made from the bones which are then incinerated and powdered. Added to fertilizers such as fish meal, it will add generous minerals to the fields. Bone broth can be canned in quart or gallon canning jars, often processed under pressure. It is the perfect base for all soups.

Streaky bacon, also referred to as side bacon, comes from the belly or side of the pig. Short cut bacon is a type of bacon that comes from the back of the pig. Middle cut bacon is a combination of both the shortcut and streaky bacon.

Hams and bacon are first submerged in brine, not unlike pickles, before canning or smoking. Typically, you use water, pickling salt, brown sugar, maple syrup, pink salt (also called Prague Powder or Modern Cure,) bay leaves, garlic and whole peppercorns. Five to seven days is usually long enough to brine both bacon and ham.

And yes, you can can bacon. You need to process jars for 75 minutes at 15 pounds of pressure, but you should first check the pressure required for your altitude. Properly canned food can retain its quality for at least a year if stored in a cool, dry place. Pressure canners work just fine on a wood stove.

Most towns in rural North America have (*Englischer*) butcher shops that usually have a meat locker. Anyone can rent space there after butchering beef, venison, pork, chicken, etc. Often, they will also process the meat for you. You just must pick up your meat regularly for use at home. Many Amish and Mennonites use propane or kerosene-powered refrigerators and freezers and store the meat in chest freezers these days.

Scrapple is a staple in Plain communities. It is typically made of hog offal such as the head, heart, liver, and other trimmings, which are boiled with any bones attached (often the entire head), to make a broth. Once cooked, bones and fat are removed, the meat is reserved, and (dry) cornmeal is boiled in the broth to make a mush. The meat, finely minced, is returned to the pot with onion added and seasonings, typically with sage, thyme, savory, black pepper, and sometimes with cinnamon, nutmeg, bay leaf, and allspice. The mush is formed into loaves and allowed to cool thoroughly until set. Then it is sliced into slabs and fried in bacon grease, oil or butter. The proportions and seasoning vary based on the region and the cook's taste. Scrapple is usually eaten as a breakfast side dish. It can be served plain or with either sweet or savory condiments: apple butter, ketchup, jelly, maple syrup, honey, or mustard.

Schnitz un Knepp (literally dried apples and dumplings) is a popular dinner main dish of ham, dried apples, and dumplings. With butchering time coming up just before the holidays, many treasured recipes are on the menu.

There are hundreds of recipes in scores of Amish cookbooks celebrating the art of cooking with pork, in all its various forms.

In *Little House on the Prairie,* Laura writes, "Pa skins the tail and skewers it on a pointed stick for Laura and Mary to roast in the hearth. As the fat drips over hot coals, Laura burns her fingers, but she is too excited to care. They ate every little bit of meat off the bones, and then they gave the bones to Jack. And that was the end of the pig's tail. There would not be another one till next year."

The last thing to go is the bladder. Scraped clean and dried, hung up by the wood stove, it is then inflated, the opening tied shut with string and can be tossed around like a ball. Thus, every part is used, nothing is wasted. Literally everything but the oink.

A little bit of oatmeal can mend almost any cooking disaster. It's the
WD-40 of the kitchen.
- Maudie, The Budget

CHAPTER 25

Good Morning Rumpumple!

Rose was lounging in bed, not relishing the thought of jumping out onto a cold wood floor with bare feet. She almost forgot it was her birthday. It had finally come. Suddenly she was being visited by Henry and Veronica singing birthday songs to her. (Yes, there are lots more beside the standard American one.)

"Happy birthday, happy birthday, may your skies be blue, may the sunshine follow you all the whole year through," her parents sang in unison. This was embarrassing. She pulled the blanket up over her head. Then it was quiet. She peeked out over the top of the quilt, and they sang again, as if on cue.

"The cock's crowing early, he is fat, round and gay, good morning Rumpumple, it's your birthday today!" They continued singing as she smiled from ear to ear, soaking up the attention.

And then another one: "Our Rosie is five today, the little birdies all are singing because it's Rosie's birthday!"

"Enough!" Rosie said, suddenly embarrassed by all the attention.

"*Chust* one more, *daumling*," Veronica promised as they dived into yet another song: "Our Rosie is five today, light the candles on the cake. Wish and quickly blow...them... OUT!"

This list goes on and on, all set to music, collected from generations of folks from all over the world.

Breakfast was festive in honor of the day: waffles with strawberries and whipped cream. The strawberries were from their own garden earlier that year. The first few pickings were eaten fresh, and then as the flats continued to be delivered to the kitchen they were turned into jellies, pies, syrups and Traffic Jam. They didn't grow their own blueberries but found good organic ones at a reasonable price at the farmers' markets in the area, one required ingredient in Traffic Jam. Again, those were eaten fresh in pies, and later turned into canned jams and syrup. Yes, it would have been a lot easier to fill all her canning jars with colored sand as Henry had suggested, but it wouldn't taste nearly as good.

Sitting at Rose's place at the table was a candy bag and a wrapped gift. Her eyes immediately went to the table as she descended the stairs into the kitchen, not noticing in the least now how cold the steps were, the wood stove not yet cranked up to capacity on this cold morning.

"Is it my new dress you've been sewing *Mamm?*" she wanted to know. "Can I open it now?" she asked.

"*May* you open it," Veronica corrected, always the teacher.

"But can I?" Rose insisted, unable to differentiate between the two yet. That would come eventually, once she went to school. Maybe. Or not.

"Yes, you may," Henry agreed. That was all the permission she needed, and she dove into the gift, ripping the paper off in bits, sending it floating to the floor.

"It is my new dress. Oh *Mamm!* Thank you!" she said as she ran around the table and hugged her mother.

Henry said then, "Looks like another package there if I'm right."

Releasing Veronica from the bear hug, she reached across the table and snagged the small package and a bit more carefully this time, unwrapped it.

"What is it?" she asked, bewildered at what she was left holding. She turned it over and over in her hands, still clueless as to what it might be.

Veronica explained. "It is a matching dress and pinafore for your dolly, Rosemary. It is all cut out and marked and you *may* sew it. I'll help you. You are old enough to learn," she added chuckling.

Rose giggled. "Really? Wow. All the things you get to do when you're five," she marveled. "What else?" she asked them then.

"Oh, I guess there's lots of things. We'll tell you when we find them. How would that be?" her father asked. Rose was thrilled and continued to giggle as she took her place at the table.

If the grass looks greener on the other side, fertilize.
~ Amish quip

Part Three

When God becomes a Child, then the wrong image of ourselves vanishes. Because in a cradle, in a crib, we see Love so small that we can pick it up. And we look at that cradle and ask ourselves, "Why do I think that God does not love me? Here He is."

~ C.D.

CHAPTER 26

White Christmas Pie

T he little calendar on Veronica's dresser didn't
disappoint this morning. How could she forget what it
said? She would revisit its wisdom several more times during
the day. This was Christmas. This is what Christmas was
meant to mean. How could it be otherwise? Forget the
Christmas trees. The lights. The lawn ornaments and Santa
and his herd of tiny adolescent reindeer. Forget the savings
one had to exhaust in order to cover all the gifts you felt
obligated to buy for every single relative and acquaintance
whom you knew would be buying gifts for you, in spite of
the fact that absolutely none of them—not a single one—
needed anything at all. Not while the rest of the Third
World were suffering and struggling in abject poverty and
need.

Do we really desire the Lord? To desire something is to be constantly
absorbed in that desire. This Advent we should go deeply into our
hearts, minds, and souls. Let us clean house and make a loving
manger for the Christ Child into which He can be born in all His
splendor. ~ C.D.

Then she thought of the baby she would have in her arms in a matter of weeks. The most incredible miracle thus far. How God had made the most horrible years of her life become the past, now a distant past she could leave behind, and her new life so terribly rich and blessed. A new daughter named Rose whom she loved to the moon and back. And a cherished husband when she was more than convinced, she could never, ever love like that again.

It is all too deep for words, Veronica reflected. *Chust impossible for us to grasp. What must heaven be like then? I can't imagine....*

Rose was in the barn with Henry 'helping' him, or so she thought, finish the Christmas presents they would bring to Canada for her cousins and aunt and uncle. She never realized those weren't her real parents. She had grown up with their *kinner,* thinking she was just one of them. And then her *dat* met Veronica and her whole world changed. Some things were better after that, like having her very own *mamm* all to herself, but she missed her brothers and sisters, who, as it turned out, were actually her cousins and not in fact siblings.

"What 'cha doing now *Dat?*" she asked Henry.

"Well, I am *chust* putting the last coat of varnish on this chess board. Their old one should have seen the wood stove years ago. We *chust* never got around to making a new one. Everything else is done and we can wrap them up now. Have you checked the chickens today? We can go by there on our way to dinner," he said.

She ignored his last suggestion, still thinking of their Christmas to-do list.

"We finished the gingerbread cookies yesterday and put them in the plastic boxes to bring up, too," she informed him. "And then we made the gingerbread *haus.* Did you see it?" Before he could answer she continued with the nonstop questions.

"How many days till we go?" Rose wanted to know. "Who is driving us up there? Will we stop for McDonalds again this time?"

"Well, Rosie, first we must have Christmas here. That's a bit over a week away. Then we can recover a couple of days from that and then go on up to *Onkel* Milo's later for *Ztvett Grischtdaag,*" he explained.

As they entered the kitchen, having removed their barn boots at the back door, Rose ran over to the dry sink pulling Henry with her.

"See? It's a gingerbread house. Look in the windows, *Dat,*" she urged.

He craned his neck as he bent down to look in the tiny windows that were carved out of the thick walls of gingerbread.

"Would you look at that!" he exclaimed, genuinely surprised.

"We cut up old cards and put the people in the windows and glued them in with icing." Pretty *schmart,* eh?" she said. "And there are cats and a dog in the other windows, too."

"Yeah," he answered, genuinely impressed. "Who taught you that?" he asked.

"*Mamm,*" she answered simply. "She knows everything."

"Well, I reckon she *chust* might," Henry wondered, his furrowed brow still puzzling this one. Rose ran to her *mamm* at the sink then and put her arms around her which didn't quite meet any longer.

"You're fat!" Rose stated, horrified, backing up a step, perplexed by this new revelation, shocked actually.

"Oh, I know," Veronica answered, quickly recovering from her surprise. She had hoped she could keep it from Rose just a bit longer.

"I, uh, guess I've been eating too many of our cookies, eh?" she said hoping it would end the discussion there.

"And Shoo-fly pie and *Yummasetti*, and *you* said you didn't want *Dat* to get *geblumpt*," Rose said crossing her arms on her chest and pouting. "I can hardly hug you now, *Mamm*," Rose complained, seriously offended.

"Maybe I'm *chust* like the animals in the woods putting on a little extra fat to keep warm in the winter," Veronica teased Rose who skipped off again singing one of her little ditties, "Hurry, hurry, hurry, we must all get fat and furry, not a moment to be lost, I can feel bold Jackie Frost..." she sang. Within minutes she was back, plying yet another thought from her seemingly endless store of questions.

"I thought you said we're gonna make a Christmas pie for Hazel and Eli for *Grischtadaag*. When are we gonna do that, *Mamm*?" she asked, coming back into the kitchen.

Veronica continued puttering at the wood stove.

"Well, I thought we could visit in a couple of days and bring them gingerbread cookies too, to have in the *haus* when people come to see them over the holidays. Some will take them out and bring them along for some visiting, but other than that they'll stay pretty close to home, I'm thinking," Veronica answered.

"Oh *gut,* then," Rose agreed. "And you'll teach me how to make it? The Christmas Pie?"

"Absolutely," Veronica reassured her, marveling that Rose seemed to have already forgotten the problem with her very expectant figure, as concerned about it as she had been only moments earlier.

Amish White Christmas Pie

There are many different recipes for White Christmas Pie. This is one of our favorites.

First, make your favorite pie dough with lard if you have any, and fill one large 9- or 10-inch pie tin, glass or metal, pressing or pinching the edges and prick with a fork. Bake. Then cool.

Filling

    1 envelope unflavored gelatin
    1/4 cup water, room temperature
    2/3 cup sugar
    1/2 teaspoon salt
    1 1/2 cups whole milk
    1/4 teaspoon almond extract
    1/4 teaspoon vanilla extract
    1/4 cup flour
    1/2 cup heavy cream
    3 egg whites
    1/4 teaspoon cream of tartar
    3/4 cups shredded coconut plus more for sprinkling over the top
    2 cups heavy or whipping cream for topping
    2 cups fresh diced strawberries
    1/2 cup powdered sugar to mix with the strawberries

Make the filling by softening the gelatin first. Put gelatin in the water in a small bowl to dissolve, not too hot. Set aside.

In a medium saucepan, mix 1/3 cup of the granulated sugar, with all of the flour and salt. Add milk and whisk to combine. Over medium heat, bring to a boil and cook one minute. Take the pan off the heat.

Add the gelatin mixture and whisk to combine over medium heat then remove from stove. Whisk in the two extracts, then place the saucepan in a bowl with ice or cold water.

Beat the ½ cup of heavy cream to soft peaks and set aside.

Beat egg whites with cream of tartar to stiff peaks, then add the remaining 1/3 cup of granulated sugar until you have stiff peaks once again and set aside.

Place the filling into a deep bowl and whisk just to make the mixture creamy.

In a large bowl, place cooled whipped filling and gently fold in whipped cream, beaten egg whites and shredded coconut. With a rubber spatula, scrape the mixture evenly into the baked pie shell.

Whip the last two cups of heavy cream to stiff peaks and using a large pastry bag with a large star tip, make a decorative top over the filling and then sprinkle some coconut over the top.

Dice strawberries and mix in a bowl with the remaining powdered sugar. The strawberries will eventually give up enough liquid and mix with the powdered sugar to create a sauce.

Cut and serve the pie with strawberry sauce on top.

By our own celebration of all the events that the will of the Lord brings to us,
we give courage and blessing to all we meet.
~ C. D.

CHAPTER 27
Help Our Unbelief

Veronica asked herself for at least the tenth time in twenty-four hours if it was foolhardy to think of travelling to Ontario for Second Christmas when she was already thirty-six weeks pregnant. She'd still be early and be home by her due date at forty weeks. And then some babies come late and arrive at forty-one or even forty-two weeks. It's up to them when they are ready, really. *No use banking on due dates. They only add stress, which no one needs*, she reminded herself, quoting her wise midwife Ruth.

Sure, it would be a break from work, not having to clean the house or cook or butcher chickens or hogs or ducks. She would be a guest and allow herself to sit and help Edith in the kitchen doing little jobs for her, peeling potatoes or chopping vegetables, or just bouncing Edith's baby on her knees, keeping Izzy happy. She remembered then what her little calendar had told her only that morning, still genuinely surprised how each entry seemed to be written just for her:

This is really the season of Mary, for she carries the Child. In

Advent the heart moves in rhythm with her life. God bent to a woman and the world heard the words: "Hail Mary, full of grace!" A girl, beholding the vision of an angel who spoke the truth. In doing so, she gave us a lesson in humility. "May it be done to me according to your word." We rejoice in Mary because she always brings us her Son. - C.D.

She concluded that all she could do was to trust in Jesus and Mary and ask for their protection during the upcoming trip. She thought to herself, *You will care for us wherever we are. We don't have to worry at all. I'll be back in plenty of time. Okay, shluss. That's sorted,* she told herself, so very tired of worrying about every little thing. It was a new time. She had to trust and let go. This wasn't helpful, fretting so. Hadn't God already proven His care beyond the shadow of a doubt? Over and over, He had dried every tear, every fear had been removed. First Henry, then a clean bill of health from the doctors and a clear go-ahead to have children, then Rose, and now a completely worry-free pregnancy. What further proof did she need? Over and above, pressed down and running over, her life had been blessed beyond her wildest dreams, and here she was still not trusting the great Creator of all things. Would she never learn? After everything that had taken place this past year. She thought to herself then, *ornery critters, that's what we are, poor, ornery ungrateful people. Won't we ever learn? How many times must He bless us before we see? Help our unbelief. Please.*

By the middle of the next day the Christmas pie was made and secure in a Tupperware pie caddy. The cookies and other offerings were boxed up as well. Today the three of them were going to visit Hazel and Eli. Veronica chided herself that they hadn't visited the old people sooner, and this was a most delayed visit, though they were kept entertained by Sarabeth who had come to look after the elderly couple. Hazel insisted that God had brought Sarabeth to them, that He knew they'd never have children and now in their old age had brought this delightful, compassionate, clever girl to be their very own. Though she would be married soon, the way most young people progressed through this stage in their life, the newlyweds were fixing up the old farmhouse on the property adjacent to Eli's own plot. Sarabeth would be close enough to include their care in her own wifely duties.

Sarabeth could hardly be described by any of the above attributes when she first came West. She was downright belligerent, resentful, wayward and obstinate, a very angry young person. Her parents tried everything over the years but were never able to find the right way with this daughter, in spite of trying valiantly.

One thing led to another and the Amish nurse, Phoebe, who had gone to college at the request of the community's bishops and obtained her nursing license, suggested that someone come to be with Faith after the terrible train crash that killed her husband and two small children. The Amish women in the community where Faith lived had made sure Faith was never alone those first months and wanted to fully support her in the aftermath of so much tragedy. They knew it would take time for her to heal. The *fraus* took turns that whole time, showing up at the farm and helping Faith maintain her life after the dreaded accident that had devastated the entire district. Phoebe's own mother had written to the girl's mother and arranged the situation, though everyone doubted it would work out and all expected they would be shipping the girl back east on the very next train to where she'd come from soon enough. But that never came to pass.

Sarabeth was Faith's *maud,* brightening up the whole place. It seemed that she blossomed in this new situation, away from judgmental parents, meddling ministers, and concerned community members. She was hardly recognizable after two years with Faith. She had surpassed everyone's expectations, but especially her own mother's, who had despaired of ever seeing her daughter happy, much less living independently someday. Marriage appeared out of the question back then. Sarabeth had refused to learn how to cook or sew, not to mention getting along with another person without bickering or all the drama she seemed to create wherever she went.

After Faith remarried and had her mother's help as they looked forward to their own growing family, Sarabeth was available to be employed again, should some needy situation warrant her help. Within days Veronica had approached Phoebe. Could Faith spare her *maud* so that Sarabeth could move in and help the aging couple? Hazel and Eli never had children of their own, much to their great disappointment and their relentless, endless prayers all those long years ago. Some of their closest friends, Veronica included, quickly realized of late, that they could no longer manage on their own. The elderly couple disagreed and thought they were coping relatively well—"*chust* fine"—according to Eli, but the facts proved differently. Quite different indeed.

The last time Veronica and Rose visited in the cozy little Handsel and Gretel *dawdi haus* things were definitely *not* under control. The sink was full of dishes from at *least* two days' worth of meals. Amish neighbors had brought a steady stream of casseroles and cakes and pies for the old couple, so they weren't suffering in that department. The place was *huddlich,* for certain.

On that last visit Veronica observed the house desperately needed cleaning. Trash cans appeared full. The wood box by the stove was running dangerously low. There were dirty clothes piling up in the wicker hampers in the washhouse connected to the main farmhouse where a cousin and his family lived, but their own eight children kept that family busy, and they hadn't exactly offered to take on the care of two elderly people besides. The garden had been abandoned over the past months, producing very little, though Hazel checked it daily for the stray green onion, a lone asparagus stalk, or radish she might find there.

Henry parked the buggy by the barn and led the horse into the enclosed paddock to join the one old nag already there, before catching up to Veronica and Rose in the house. The old couple were already seated at the kitchen table, visiting. Sarabeth was pulling down pie plates and mugs from the hutch cupboard and counting out spoons and forks, reheating the coffee from that morning and pouring some cream into a little pitcher.

Meanwhile, Veronica was scanning the kitchen, unable to detect even the tiniest sign of the chaos she had encountered only the month before. *Sink, gut; windows washed... check.* Veronica went down the list in her head. *Dish towels drying on the wooden spider by the stove-check. Wood box filled, check. Trash cans dumped, yes. Laundry walking out of the clothes hampers on their own, nope. Looks like the laundry is caught up, too. Tinder ready by the wood box, check. Pots and pans hanging up, the Paul Revere copper bottoms even polished to a sheen. Oh, my,* Veronica thought to herself. *I could use Sarabeth for a couple of weeks, too. Who would have guessed? Not in a million years....*

"So *gut* of you to *kumm,*" Hazel was saying. "Uh, Sara," Hazel called then. "Please bring out that Shoo-fly *bief* in the pantry. We'll save the Christmas *bief* they brought for another day, eh? It needs to be *geendt* up. And if there is any of that whipped topping in the ice box?"

"Okay," Sarabeth happily agreed while setting the pie plates on the table along with a pie server and a knife.

Rose sat on the bench, her feet crossed, swinging back and forth. Rosemary sat on her lap wearing her new dress that matched Sarabeth's. She was tightly wrapped up in the dolly quilt. This dress and pinafore were teal. She was quiet, remembering what her *mamm* told her earlier: that children were to be seen and not heard, especially when visiting out, except when they are spoken to directly.

Hazel smiled across the table at Rose.

"Did you help make the White Pie?" Hazel queried.

"Oh, yes," Rose answered. "And the snowflakes and the cookies." She raced on without taking a breath. "I can put the snowflakes up for you, too, if you want, I brought tape along...." She forged full speed ahead with all that was bottled up inside her, but now that she had been asked finally, she thought she had permission to wax eloquently. "The snowflakes are made outta white *kaffi* filters. *Mamm* showed me how...." Rose abruptly stopped talking mid-sentence when she looked over at Veronica and realized what the tight lips and the frown meant: she should stop right there. She had answered beyond enough. But Hazel found it delightful. She missed seeing children so much, except when she went to church but that was only every other week and most of them there weren't sitting still. The smaller ones at least. They were chasing after each other, squealing with delight, running through the house and back outside, around the barns and through the fields. A civil conversation was out of the question. If Hazel got lucky, one of the mothers might ask her to hold her infant while she helped with the lunch. That kind usually slept in her arms, but even that was just fine with her.

The children next door were in school most of the week and when not there, were tending to their chores. Reading was a luxury they seldom had time for. They didn't get homework since the parents in the district had approached the teacher and explained that they had enough work once they got home, chores and exercising the horses, emptying the ashes from all the wood stoves into the hod with the small metal shovel, the girls catching up on the laundry and helping with the baking. With a family that size they baked twice a week, helping out with the youngest children when their *mamm* couldn't.

Have we made the doors of the stables of our hearts secure against the cold winds of apathy, selfishness, indifference, so that these cannot penetrate? Is the dry wood of our sacrifices, our penances, our prayers, ready to be lit to provide warmth for the Child in that cold stable?
~ C. D.

CHAPTER 28
Honey Dew

Rose quickly resumed her children-should-only-be-seen-and-not-heard diminutive pose on the bench. Her lips were sealed. She smoothed out her dress and pinafore over her knees. Then she folded her hands on her lap over Rosemary's middle as she lay across Rose's knees. She again crossed her ankles.

Sarabeth brought the dishes to the table and set them down near Veronica where she noticed Veronica's expansive middle.

"Oh! I didn't know..." she began happily, but not before Veronica frowned, quite fiercely it seemed, and raised her chin indicating Rose.

"Oh. I...um...okay," Sarabeth hurriedly switched gears. Then Hazel, who was privy to this awkward moment cut in.

"Sarabeth," Hazel quickly interjected. "Why don't you take Rose out to the barns and show her the guinea pigs? She'd like that."

"Oh. Sure. I can do that," she answered, taking Rose by the hand and heading out the kitchen door.

"*Kumm* back for snack when you're done," Hazel added.

When they were gone Hazel let out an audible sigh. "Sorry about that," she apologized to Veronica.

"It's fine. We've managed to keep it under wraps so far. On a different note, we're planning to go to Henry's family for *Ztvett Grischtdaag*."

"Oh, that will be fun. For sure you won't be going away much after he *kumms*," Hazel noted, looking down at Veronica's girth.

Then Eli spoke, quite energized by the visitors.

"So how is married life treating you?" he asked Henry.

"Oh, it's all honey dew," Henry answered sweetly.

"Um, what 'cha mean?" Eli asked, a bit perplexed.

"It's all, 'honey do this' and 'honey do that,'" Henry chuckled at his own joke.

"Oh, that's a new one," Eli said and joined in the laughter. "Ya, I like that one." It took Hazel another minute to get the joke. Then she started laughing too.

When Sarabeth and Rose went outside, they could see the two barns. One housed their neighbor's guinea pig industry, worked primarily by the children. The little critters needed clean bedding daily, and fresh water and more grain. Petting each guinea pig was also required. A proper visit on one of the children's laps, every single day, for every single guinea pig without fail, included brushing and playing with each one. No pet store or prospective buyer would want one that had not grown up being socialized and used to being around children. Should one of them miss that stage in their early development, it would most likely go into 'fight or flight' mode when held.

All animals protect themselves using the fight-or-flight or fight-flight-freeze-and-play-dead as a physiological reaction that occurs in response to a perceived attack, or threat to survival. Sarabeth found out the hard way the previous year when she was in town and visited a pet store. One very cute little Russian hamster breed bit her finger when she picked it up, and the thing would not let go. The owner of the store could not get it to unlatch while Sarabeth's blood continued dripping onto the floor, so he brought a bucket of water and had Sarabeth lower her hand into it, still attached to the little guy. Then he did let go, now resembling a wet rat, and was promptly returned to his cage before he could bite anyone else or drown. Needless to say, he could not be sold as a pet. He'd already flunked the adoption test.

The other barn was full to capacity. Sarabeth gave Rose the grand tour. The horses' stalls were near the forebay so they could be taken out quickly. Next came the milking cows and the goats. There was a ready market for raw cows' milk and fresh goat milk in the area. The hay was piled to the ceiling in the loft on the second story and was carried there through the back door stationed on an artificial 'hill' that had been created just for this task. The apex of the hill was level with the door, making it all the way up to the second level. Tacked onto the back corner of the barn were the pigs.

Their shed had a revolving door so that they could go out to their little fenced area in their yard and play in the mud and snuffle through their slops out there, too. It contained a water trough also. A farrowing fence built along one side of the indoor enclosure is called their 'zone' and is small enough for new piglets to escape through but far too small for a sow. It allows a safe alternative for the piglets when their mother decides a nap is in order and literally throws herself onto her side, resembling a beached whale, often smothering the young pigs. Pigs of any size are a valuable commodity, and a farmer can't risk losing any of them at all. An average size sow can easily top two hundred, and eighty pounds and they have been known to have as many as fourteen piglets in one litter, called a 'drove.' Surviving piglets learn quite early where to escape to when Mother decides to have a lie-down.

Rose wanted to go back and hold the guinea pigs some more, but Sarabeth said they should get to the house. The two of them headed back then. Sarabeth stood with her bare feet soaking in the wash basin on the grass by the door. A quick scrub with the brush provided there ensured that they wouldn't be bringing anything they'd encountered on the barn floor back into the house. Rose followed suit and also scrubbed her feet in the water, forgetting to hold the hem of her dress up which became quite soaked.

Just as they were coming into the kitchen, Hazel was telling her guests about the impending wedding. They washed their hands at the chore sink and sat down to eat their pie, the wet hem dripped onto the floor under the table. The others had already finished.

Hazel continued. "We're going back East for the wedding. It is all so exciting."

Then Eli added, "I don't remember the last time I went East."

Hazel reminded him. "Oh, you don't remember? We went to Pinecraft, uh, what was it now? Ten years ago?"

Eli replied then, "Oh, right. That big yellow barn had the market there, bakery, restaurant, best coconut cream pie on earth, too. How could I forget? Ya, now I remember."

Eli continued, "They are quite famous for that pie, I

heard. Yup, that was the time you talked me into that two-seater kayak thingy—whatever it was called—and you saw something in the water and thought it was an alligator and leaned too far over to look at it and we baled; youse was screaming yer head off. We had on life jackets, ya know, got back on land pretty quick," he chuckled while Hazel frowned and shook her head.

"I thought that was the end for us. It wasn't funny either! Don't laugh. I could have died from a heart attack, youse!" Hazel raised her voice at Eli.

"But you didn't, did you? And you weren't eaten by an alligator, either," Eli noted calmly, still enjoying this banter.

"No, I didn't. Only because the guardian angels protected us," she countered.

"You did enjoy the rest of the month there," Eli reminded her. "We never got to canoeing or to Disney Land," he teased.

"Hmff," Hazel told him what she thought about that. "Ya, but not in the water. Never again. I'm not going near water for the rest of my life, mind you," Hazel grumped. Eli tried to hide his giggle behind his hand.

"Yeah, and I thought you was *chust* trying to save water here. I wouldn't recommend cutting out your weekly bath, though. It is becoming hard to ignore, dear," Eli suggested.

"*Shluss,* youse!" Hazel tried to hush him. This was getting downright embarrassing.

Pinecraft is a Plain community sitting on the edge of the city of Sarasota, Florida. During the heat of the summer, Pinecraft is home to several hundred Amish and Mennonite people, who call the place home. During the colder winter months, Pinecraft comes alive with thousands of Amish and

Mennonite visitors who go seeking a break from farming or building furniture in their frigid northern communities. During December, January, and February, Amish and Mennonites from all over the United States and Canada call Pinecraft home for a little while. Some hire long-distance taxi vans to transport them, but the majority arrive on Greyhound buses or Amtrak trains. It seems there are no horses and buggies in the little town but instead three-wheel bikes and golf carts which are quickly mastered.

The only real stumbling block is the fear of failure. When it comes to cooking, straighten your apron and chase your dreams.
~ Maudie, The Budget

CHAPTER 29
Gratitude

In Milverton, Ontario, Milo's family were caught up in the Christmas spirit. There were more school 'snow days' this time of year in Canada. Blizzard after blizzard kept them home more often than not. That was just fine with them. The children spent hours when they weren't in school drawing and coloring Christmas cards. It was getting late to mail them, but then it was okay if they didn't arrive until Second Christmas, over a week after First Christmas. Their friends and family would still be celebrating.

The children were equally busy making homemade gifts for each other. They didn't know Uncle Henry and Aunt Veronica and Rose planned a surprise visit for Second Christmas, but their parents encouraged them to think of Rose and suggested making her some gifts, too. It was only a little 'white lie' if Milo let the children know he would mail them to Rose to enjoy for Christmas. He and Edith had managed to keep the visit under wraps so far. In a busy household, it didn't attract much notice if extra sheets were added to the laundry pile or if the pantry seemed especially well stocked, or if their mother seemed to be baking more bread or cookies and cakes than usual. It was Christmas, for goodness' sake!

The kitchen was plenty warm. Edith was busy making breakfast. Izzy, the baby, was having her morning nap along with two-year old Louie. Four-year old Lenny and five-year old Ruby were throwing their whole little souls into the important task they had been assigned. They were coloring brown paper with crayons. When one sheet was filled, Edith quickly replaced it with another. She would use these to wrap the gifts for their cousins. She praised them for their beautiful wrapping paper, hoping it would keep them busy for a while longer. Store-bought silver and gold star stickers were also added to their drawings. This was serious work. They looked forward to it all year long. They thrived on that.

As the children sat at the long table and busily worked on their wrapping paper, gifts and cards, they talked among themselves about what they were wishing for come Christmas. They had, on occasion, gone with one parent or the other on those rare shopping trips to Target or Walmart and marveled at all the shelves there overflowing with toys.

Edith stood at the stove thinking that she'd heard plenty and decided that was more than enough time for the children to be dreaming and wishing for gifts for themselves.

"Listen up," she began. "Youse all been thinking here about all the things you want when it would be far better, and less selfish, to think of all the things you are grateful for. You are better off than most *kinner* in the whole world, ya know. You've seen that magazine–*A Common Place*—that *Dat* gets about the missions where the Mennonites go to help people in other lands. Why, many of those children don't have clean drinking water or a change of clothes, much less enough to eat. You should think about being grateful, not what you want. Our simple life is about living with what

Gott has given us and thinking of others." The children looked down then, rightly chastised, understanding exactly what their mother wanted them to consider.

"But how can we help them, *Mamm*, the children who need so much?" Lester asked.

"Well, I thought we should gather some things at the thrift stores and write letters and I've written to that mission organization asking for an address for a family that might like to get to know us and write to us. I haven't heard back yet. They might find us a family anywhere in the world, Africa or Bolivia or China even," Edith explained. "Organizations like that often send whole semi-trailers full of donations. We can send it to their shipping dock to add to the next trailer going by sea. When it's full it will sail to a country in need and their workers on the other side will distribute it all. When I was about your age our family 'adopted' a family in The Gambia, in Africa. We exchanged letters and they even sent a photo of their family. It doesn't feel like a lot, but they knew someone was thinking of 'em and we hoped they felt the love and prayers."

"That would be so cool!" Lester said. The others all nodded in agreement. "I can't wait for that," Lester added.

"Can you send me in the trailer? I've always wanted to see those countries," Abby asked.

Ruby, who always copied her big sister, also weighed in. "Me, too."

"Can I become a missionary when I grow up?" Lester wanted to know.

"'Most anything is probably possible," his mother replied, though she wasn't aware of any Amish *youngie* having done that to date.

Then Edith remembered something Veronica had written in a letter recently. It so impressed her that she cut it out and tacked it to the wall above her dresser:

. . .

Making friends with a lonely or unloved child is to bring Christ to that little one. Take the child into your heart. When you do, you take Christ into your heart. Surely in eternity He will reverse the process by taking you into His Heart. ~ C.D.

Edith had been the first one to rise that morning. With dawn slowly lighting the house she picked up any objects left around from the night before. She gathered the dirty laundry from the hampers, then hurried downstairs, depositing it all in the *kesselhaus* by the root cellar and stoked the fire under the canning kettles already filled with water and sitting on the wood stove there. Before she hurried up the stairs, she grabbed a quart jar of maple syrup from the shelves in the root cellar that they had canned early last spring after the maple syrup run which peaked in February. Then she checked the firebox on the cookstove, jiggling the grate to let the ash settle down below and expose the glowing coals that remained on the grate from the fire the night before. She carefully added wood on top of the coals and opened the damper, letting air in to fuel a roaring blaze. Next, she gathered the leftovers from the projects on the kitchen table and stored those on the other side of the kitchen with the wrapping paper and all else the children had been working on.

She pulled back the blue curtains on three sides of the kitchen, securing them with clothes pins. The chill was starting to wear off as she set a cast iron griddle over two of the four iron plates on the cookstove to heat. Then she went into the pantry off the kitchen returning with eggs, flour, corn meal, buckwheat flour and the jug of milk she had set there the night before to curdle. She added a nob of leftover bacon drippings from the crock in the pantry and the now-turned buttermilk. Mixing it all together in her large tin bread bowl, she whisked in a pinch each of salt and baking soda. Setting that aside, she found the large ladle she was looking for standing upright in the crock with the other numerous utensils on the shelf by the cookstove.

Slowly the sleepy children came down the stairs, rubbing their eyes.

"What day are we on, *Mamm*," Lester asked looking up on the calendar on the wall by the sink.

"Day eighty-seven," she answered.

"A hundred days till Christmas sure goes slow," Abby sighed. Abby was seven.

"Slow," Ruby, who was five, agreed without looking up while swatting her unruly hairs from her face. Ruby followed everything Abby said or did.

"*Mamm* says we gotta be patient," Abby said to Ruby.

"What's the picture on the Advent calendar today?" Ruby wanted to know.

"It's my turn to open the little door," Lenny yelled and looked up from his coloring. He had already resumed his place at the table to continue what he had been so engrossed in the day before. Slipping off his chair he dragged it across the barnwood floor to the opposite side of the kitchen and climbed up on it. Edith put down the spoon she was using and ran barefoot over to Lenny as he teetered on the chair, looking for door number fifteen. Finding the right one, he carefully pulled on the little tab to open it and stared at the picture.

"What is it, *Mamm?*" he asked, bewildered.

"It's from the Christmas carol 'A Partridge in a Pear Tree,' you know the verse, 'Ten Lords a Leaping.' You know that one, eh?" she asked as she grabbed him around the middle and lowered him to the floor.

"Leaping, leaping," he called as he skipped and hopped round and round the kitchen, deciding this was far more fun than coloring some more.

"I am grateful for my home, having food, and my healthy *kinner*," Edith said while flipping eight pancakes at a time in succession, lined up on the griddle, hoping to turn the conversation around to gratitude and not selfish wishing, though they were children, but it was her task to lead them to God and instill the importance of the true meaning of Christmas.

"I'm grateful for the wooden barn *Doddy* made for my toy horses last year," Lenny said. That reminded Lester of what his *Doddy* and *Grossmammi* had given him.

"I got that *wunderbar* toy truck and horse trailer that it hooked up to," he said, which reminded Edith of the hours of fun the boys (and girls) had together shipping their little horses from one end of the house to the opposite far end and back again all day long. The only drawback to that memory was that she had what seemed an overabundance of knees to mend in the boys' trousers that year, worn and threadbare having pushed the vehicles back and forth for hours on their hands and knees.

"But the best thing last year was the bow and arrows you and *Dat* gave me. And I passed my safety test for it, too," Lester beamed.

"I am grateful for Alice who pulls us *kinner* on the sled around and around the fields," Abby said. And then more to herself she added, "I bet Alice will be glad when sledding season is over. She's gotta be one tired horse, for sure."

"Sleigh rides!" Ruby agreed with Abby.

"My best Christmas thing when I was little was *kumming* down the stairs and seeing the table in the morning, all covered with presents and each place had a plate with sweets and candies, and I tried, but I *chust* couldn't eat only one candy a day, though that's what I'd planned on," Milo said, chuckling as he came into the kitchen from the barn. Then he added, "Oh, and the book *Doddy* gave me, *The Education of Little Tree* by Forrest Carter. I must have read that a dozen times since then. I think I should find my copy and read it to youse all. Oh, and they also gave me that other one, *Where the Red Fern Grows* by Wilson Rawls about a boy who buys and trains two Redbone Coonhounds for hunting. Boy, was that a *gut* book."

"But we're getting away from gratitude here," Edith said, glaring at Milo with 'that look,' hoping that he'd get the message that she was trying to steer the conversation back on track, away from the materialism that threatened to sabotage a sacred Christmas celebration. But she quickly found herself overcome with nostalgia and the memories came flooding back to her, too. She continued as she piled pancakes onto the platter on the cooler side of the stove top.

"My favorite memory of Christmas was going to *Grossmammi* and *Doddy's dawdy haus* and they would sit in their rocking chairs by the stove and pass out candy to all of us."

"My other favorite part is each year seeing you *kinner* in front of all the parents at school putting on the Christmas program. I look forward to that all year long," Milo chimed in, in spite of himself.

"And one year my *Mamm,* your other *grossmammi,* got the whole *Little House on the Prairie* set of books that we're still reading at bedtime all these years since," Edith remembered.

"Will we put out our stockings again this year?" Lester asked.

"Yes!" Lenny yelled, still leaping around the room with the ten lords.

"Who fills them?" Abby asked.

"Well," Milo began. "Some say the angels *kumm* on Christmas Eve," he ventured.

"And some *kinner* at church told me Santa does," Abby explained. "But he isn't real or is he?" she wanted to know.

Edith tackled this one. "It all *kumms* from a legend long ago, and we weren't there so we don't know how true the story is, I guess, but they say a very good and holy man named Nicholas would make sure all the poorest children got Christmas presents and enough food and he would leave everything at their houses, but no one ever really saw him doing it, but they all got lots of *gut* things every Christmas in that land."

Then Milo asked, "Do you remember us reading about Mr. Edwards in *Little House on the Prairie* who showed up on Christmas Eve all wet and cold having ford the creek leading to the Ingall's house and told Mary and Laura that he knew ancient old St. Nicholas would never make it across the flooded creek so he offered to deliver the gifts for him?"

"But that is how all legends are born, I guess," Edith pondered.

"I vote we put up stockings anyway and see what happens," Lester stated decisively.

Milo laughed. "This isn't exactly a democracy. But it is okay to try it I guess," he said, looking over at Edith. She nodded ever so slightly in answer to his response. Then, shaking herself, she addressed the gathering in the kitchen in a loud voice.

"Okay, youse all. Clean up, please. Pancakes are ready. *Chust* set your projects on the sideboard, and we'll work on it all again later. Breakfast is ready," she said washing her hands and quickly drying them on her kitchen apron. While Lester wiped down the oil cloth on the long table, Abby went about setting the places. The condiments' tote was returned to the center of the table and the plates and bowls stacked at the end by the wood stove from where *Mamm* would serve them. Glasses were filled with water and teacups gathered on the stove top on the right, away from the hotter side of the stove. Silverware was distributed at each place.

Right on time they could hear Izzy waking up as Louie ran into the kitchen soon after, now energized by his nap. Edith ran into the bedroom and scooped up Izzy. She brought her down to the kitchen and deposited the happy baby in the cradle by the table where she could hear and see her family. Just as Edith unwrapped the blanket around the baby, their calico cat, 'Orange-y', jumped into the cradle, jealous of the attention the little one was getting.

Without a word Abby slid off the bench, lifted and then whisked the cat out the kitchen door, dumping her on the back step with a firm "*kst!*" letting the door bang shut.

"Wash your hands please," Edith called to her.

I suggest that for Advent, the days leading up to Christmas, we remove from our vocabularies, our conversations, our thoughts and, if possible, from our dreams the sentences: 'I feel,' 'I want,' and 'I would like' and that we replace them with: 'What does God want of me?'
~ C.D.

CHAPTER 30
Hallicher Grischtdaag!

It was an every-other-Sunday-off church day so they could sleep in later, which was a rare enough occurrence. The house was silent. The cows wouldn't be too happy should they have to wait much longer to be milked but Henry would be out there soon enough.

The night before, after Rose was in bed and sound asleep, he snuck out to the barn and came back to the kitchen door as Veronica was pouring their nightly ritual mugs of steaming cocoa.

"What are you doing out there?" she startled when he stepped into the kitchen through the doorway.

"Close your eyes," he whispered.

"What is it?" Veronica insisted.

"*Chust* close your eyes, eh?" he repeated.

"Okay. They're closed," she answered, growing impatient. "Is it alive, then?" she queried.

"Nope," was all he offered. She could hear him shuffling across the kitchen floor until he was almost in front of her.

"Ooo...kaaay," he said. She slowly opened her eyes, not sure what she'd find there.

"Oh my! Henry! You didn't. You did. When did you do that? When did you have time? And Rose doesn't know either?" she questioned him.

"Nope. She didn't take it in at all," he laughed. "Just another project at the work bench."

"Why, it's a beauty!" she exclaimed as she ran her hand over the beautiful glossy wooden hood on the maple cradle.

"*Hallicher Grischtdaag!*" Henry said as he bent to kiss her. She wrapped her arms around him (as best she could manage.)

"Thank you so much. It is beautiful. Very unexpected, too. You really surprised me," she said.

"I was thinking, we could put it in the bedroom and pile all the presents in it and just tell her it's for holding everything ready for the trip to Canada," he suggested.

"I hope she'll go for that," she answered. "We can try."

The next morning dawned. They stayed where they had awakened only a moment before, noses touching, hands entwined. Opening his eyes Henry whispered, "It's our first Christmas together, ya know."

"You're right. It's so special. We'll always look back fondly to these days," Veronica said.

She tried to roll over, which was neigh impossible without help.

"*Chust* stay here a minute," he smiled. "It's so quiet."

"Mmmmm," she agreed.

"Tomorrow is Christmas Eve," he said.

"And then it all begins. Visitors, church, more visitors, going out, hyper *kinner* from all the cookies and candy," she voiced.

"Ya," he agreed reluctantly. "But then we get ready for

176

Canada. Then you can relax. All the gifts are made already, you don't need to bake anything else. We're pretty much packed. The barn is covered. We really can *chust* enjoy today and tomorrow and Christmas. They'll be caroling tomorrow, the *youngie*. Rose will enjoy that. She might even remember it from last year at Milo's. I'll help make the cocoa for the carolers and serve it when the sleighs *kumm* by. You don't have to do anything. Nothing at all. Really. *Chust* watch from the rocking chair."

Then as an afterthought he added, "Why don't you stay here in bed. I'll make breakfast. No, really. I mean it. Me and Rose will. She'll love that."

"If you insist," Veronica laughed. She wasn't about to protest such an invitation as that.

"I'll milk first, it won't take long. You can go back to sleep." he said, throwing back the covers on his side of the bed. He quickly dressed and came back to the bed, startling her awake with a gentle playful pat. "*Shlaff gut*," he whispered as he left.

Behold a donkey, a girl and a man walking alone, travelling light in the starry night. Let's go join them and see why so much ecstasy surrounds them.
~ C.D.

CHAPTER 31

Christmas Chutney

S arabeth was growing impatient. "I can't read this, it's *chust* too small!" she complained.

"Ya, my *mamm's* writing was really tiny. Here, let me try." Hazel took the recipe card from Sarabeth.

"You should go to that nice doctor in town and have your eyes checked. These new glasses of mine are the cat's pajamas!" Hazel said as she skimmed the card.

Sarabeth started laughing at that and couldn't stop. "Where in the world did you get *that* expression? That's *insch!*" she howled.

"Oh, something us girls used to say in school," Hazel chuckled at Sarabeth's reaction.

"Okay. I think Eli got everything last week when he went with that driver to the stores. It took a lot of looking but he eventually found it all. The health food store had most of it. We can make up enough to bring to each place we visit at *Grischtdaag*, and we can wrap the little jars in calico cloth with a ribbon. That'll be pretty. We can make plenty to have for anyone *kumming* here to visit, too. Oh! I am so glad I can pass this on to you. Otherwise *Mamm's* recipe could be lost forever," Hazel said as her eyes teared up. Finding her handkerchief, she dried her eyes and looked at Sarabeth.

"My *Dat* tells the story that years ago a missionary from India came to speak at one of those Mennonite revival things, though I don't hear much about them anymore, but *Mamm* and *Dat* invited him home with them afterwards for dinner. Was he ever shocked to find Indian chutney on the table. He ate most of the jar. He kept telling her it was as *gut* as or even better than the chutney they make in India. She said she found it in a book once and wrote it down. It's *gut* with chicken and rice. That's what she fixed for him that night. She sent him home with several jars, too."

"And it's called Amish Christmas Chutney?" Sarabeth wondered.

"Ya. A bit of a mystery, isn't it?" Hazel asked.

Then Hazel said, "I'll read it all off and you tell me if we have everything, okay?"

She began: "Ingredients, are ya ready?" Hazel asked.

"Ya, I'm ready. *Chust* read," Sarabeth urged her on.

"Okay. Four Beef tomatoes, large,"

"Check," Sarabeth concurred.

"2 sticks Celery."

"Yes," she answered.

Hazel continued, going through the whole list.

"1 – 2 nobs fresh Ginger root, peeled and thinly sliced."

"Check."

"2 Green bell peppers"

"Check."

"2 White onions, large"

"Yes."

"1 whole lime, peeled and pitted."

"Ya."

"1 heaping tablespoon grated lime zest."

And so it went as Sarabeth located all the ingredients in order.

"3/4 tsp Allspice, ground
1/2 tsp Black pepper, ground
1/2 tsp Celery seed
1 tsp Cinnamon, ground
1 tsp Cloves, ground
1/2 tsp Salt
¼ cup Apple cider vinegar.

Two cups of sugar, brown, white, or honey, and salt to taste."

"I have seen most recipes for chutney calling for green tomatoes or tomatillos," Hazel explained. "I sometimes add green apples, curry powder, coriander and cumin, so I made sure we had those too, this time around," Hazel explained. "I remember now, once my *mamm* put in golden raisins. That was *abbeditlich* for sure!"

"Yup, we're *gut* to go," Sarabeth pronounced.

"Well, we'll wash and chop and peel it all and then mix it in the big bread bowl. Then it gets sent through the large die on the meat grinder. Then we *chust* boil it all together for about ten minutes, scraping the bottom of the pot so it doesn't scorch, if I remember correctly, keeping it as hot as we can. You keep it hot too, while you fill the jars. Then you taste it. It is supposed to be 'too hot, ya know, spicy to stand, and too sweet to resist.' That's what they say in India about chutney, the missionary told us. Then we get the jelly jars hot in the oven or the water bath, fill them with chutney and wipe off the rims. Then you screw on the lids and set them all upside down to cool. You can also use a water bath. About 20 minutes for half pints. I'm thinking this recipe won't make much. We can figure out how to multiply the measurements if we need to. *Mamm* often had to do that. How's your math, Sarabeth?"

By dusk, when you really can't see well enough anymore, and you'd finally succumbed to the inevitable—lighting the lamps—the last batch of jars were being wiped down and the lids capped on. Then they were turned upside down on a towel that had been laid out on the last free space on the table. It wasn't a very big table anyway, being in the small *dawdi haus,* built for only two people.

"We'll do the pots and all in the morning," Hazel proposed. "And tie on the cloth and ribbons. Then they'll all be ready."

Eli called from the sitting room right off of the tiny kitchen.

"Is there any *zapper* tonight? Or is chutney all I'll be getting?" he asked, not exactly joking.

"Oh, ye of little faith," his wife replied. "Your *dochder* made your favorite. It will be done soon. However, we might have to get out the TV trays and eat in *die gut shtup.* We've run outta room here, I'm afraid."

"Why are they called 'TV trays' anyway?" Sarabeth chuckled.

"The English use them, I'm guessing, for eating their *zapper* while they watch their TVs," Hazel explained. "*Chust* the right height to eat at. That's what the label said at the dollar store where I found them. 'TV trays,' it said. I knew they'd *kumm* in handy someday."

"I'll get the mac and cheese outta the oven. It should be ready 'bout now," Sarabeth said.

We are not promised skies always blue, but a Helper to see us through.
- Amish saying

CHAPTER 32

Grischtdaagnacht

C hristmas Eve. Hallowed in every conceivable dwelling for over two-thousand years: a stable, in hovels crowded with the poor of the earth, mansions of the rich, a cold garret, a palace, a cave, a loft—wherever the Baby is longed for, expectantly awaited. Wherever and whenever humanity hoped and prayed for true peace and true brotherhood, the Baby King could surely bring that to our poor suffering masses. We need only to pray and believe.

Amish *youngie* sing their hearts out on Christmas Eve: old hymns, contemporary ballads, and modern carols. All over North America, Amish young people pile onto sleighs that they have kept ready in their barns all year, waiting for this holy night.

Christmas Eve. Candles are burning in the windows where families are waiting to be courted by the sleigh-loads of happy youth. The next generation. These souls are the Amish Church's hope and prayer for the future. These sleighs represent a hard fought-for battle to live out what they believe. Their ancestors were martyred for those beliefs. They were driven across countries and continents in their search for a place of peace where they could continue their beloved way of life. And they have managed to do just that, in spite of Father Time pushing ahead in the world's greedy grab for prosperity, power and domination. For millennia the good fight has been fought. The troops are gathering now once more, teaching what they would live and die for to their heirs, some of whom understand the epic spiritual battle being waged, while others are oblivious, so they must fight on, bringing all back into the fold, into the Church.

"Is it Christmas Eve yet, *Dat?*" Rose wanted to know.

"Yes, and I hear sleigh bells already," he confirmed as they stood in the window facing the main road. "There they are. They're *kumming!*" Henry pointed toward the rise in the road leading up to their farm.

"And I can open the door and pass out mugs and you'll give them cocoa and peppermint sticks?" Rose recited.

"Yes, that's the plan," Veronica said from her rocking chair which they'd brought to the bay window earlier.

For the next two hours the sleighs pulled up to the house one after another and the *youngie* spilled out onto the yard singing one carol after another. Then gulping down the steamy cocoa, they returned the mugs with hearty wishes for a *gut Grischtnacht* and piled back into their sleighs. The bells could still be heard as the next sleigh could be seen mounting the hill to their house. They reigned in their team of horses, and once more the carolers sang their hearts out, drank cocoa, wished all a very *Hallicher Grischtdaagnacht* and were off once more.

Finally, after waiting for more than fifteen minutes, Henry suggested they get ready for bed. It was very late and most likely the carolers were home with their families by now. Even Rose was wilting at this point. She knew she'd want to be up early for Christmas morning, so she changed for bed and brushed her teeth without even being asked. The little family gathered in the master bedroom where Henry read the Christmas story from the children's Bible once again. Veronica led Rose to her room and tucked her in. She was asleep as soon as Veronica pulled up the quilt. She stood there gazing at the child. *So many blessings, Gott. So much love has been poured on us. It's overwhelming. Denki. Denki. It's too deep for words,* she thought, shaking her head.

She touched the long stocking Rose had hung on the bed post earlier. *If I don't do it now, I'll forget for sure,* she told herself. Taking the stocking she went back downstairs and found what she was looking for in the kitchen pantry. She dropped in a little Clementine tangerine that she had hidden there earlier in the day into the sock. Next went in a kiwi. After that a pomegranate, exotic fruits reminding them of the lands where the kings must have hailed from and where the Baby was born. After that went in a handful of peanuts still in their shells. She reached back up to the shelf there and found the candy canes she had Henry get the last time he went out shopping. The candy canes were sticking out of the top of the long sock. She couldn't get anything else in it if she tried. Then she turned to the large tin pie keeper with its nail-punched pineapple design on the front door and took out the three plates of goodies she had assembled the day before. She carefully placed those at their places on the table. Red candles were already set on a white linen tablecloth. She and Rose had made a center-piece earlier in the week, too. A platter sat in the middle of the table with pinecones, a sprig of holly with its red berries and the little white-onyx donkey figurine Veronica received when she was five, and always brought out for Christmas.

Some Amish communities allowed Nativity scenes with kings and shepherds and the Holy Family, but in their settlement, a donkey and candles and sprigs of holly would do just fine.

Veronica pulled herself back up the stairs by the banister and finally climbed into bed, winded by the effort. Henry was already snoring. She gazed at him in the moonlight as it bathed his face. *So dear, so many blessings, Gott. Denki. Denki.*

Advent and pregnancy are times of waiting, times of the great prayer of silence that we women know, times of utter humility and holy tranquility, of a strange union with God the Father, from Whom all paternity comes. They are times of living with Mary and learning from her all there is to learn about expectant motherhood, and about motherhood fulfilled.
~ C.D.

CHAPTER 33
Sleigh Bells

Christmas Eve in Ontario was very similar to Rose's back in the States. Carolers, last minute preparations, reading from the children's Bible, and lots of goodies suddenly appearing, though only a preface to the coming of Second Christmas' abundance and celebrations in only another ten days' time.

"*Dat,* please let me go on the next sleigh. I promise they'll bring me straight back home afterwards. Please?" Lester begged.

"Okay, but you'll still be up for milking tomorrow, got that?" Milo asked.

"Oh, yes!" Lester agreed as he pulled on his snow boots and parka, wool cap and mittens. Edith grabbed a scarf from the clothes tree by the door and wrapped it around his neck before he could jump out the door and down the steps to join the sleigh. It would be his first year caroling. A veritable right-of-passage for any *Amische youngie.*

Close to three hours later he came bounding in the kitchen door. The children had all been put to bed already and Milo and Edith were sitting at the table cracking peanuts from a bowl and sipping cocoa.

"How did it go?" Milo asked as Lester peeled off layers of clothes caked with snow.

"It was *wunderbar-gut!* People gave us cookies and cake and cocoa and then we'd go to the next farm, and it would be the same thing all over again. And guess who was on our sleigh? My friend Mose from school got to go with his older brother Toby, and our cousin Dorcas, and Aunt Lucy. We had such a *gut* time! Then some went skating and we stood around the bonfire there a bit. They were passing out S'mores, but I said I had to get home, and they were bringing others back then too. It was great fun. Thanks so much I could go," he said as he grabbed a handful of peanuts and sat down with them.

"We did see one sleigh that flipped out on County Road Nine on that big curve. The horses must have thought the edge of the road was farther away and drove right into a ditch filled with snow. No one was hurt, but we stayed to help turn it back upright. They were lucky. The horses weren't too spooked after that. They drove them slower, though."

"Well, I'm done in, good night all," Edith announced as she got up. She and Milo had assembled the plates that would sit at each child's place and had them lined up on the sideboard. Milo planned to put them on the table before he went out to the barn in the morning.

The children had spent several afternoons making little acorn people out of acorns they'd collected before the first snow, fashioning arms and legs out of toothpicks. (It helps to puncture the acorn with an embroidery needle before inserting a toothpick.) A black marker is used to draw little faces, mostly happy, though someone always sneaks in an angry-looking face, or turned-down mouth. The acorn centerpiece almost reached from one end of the long table to the other. The dozen or so little 'people' were standing on a long moss-covered plank of bark, with little mushrooms, flowers, and miniature bridges and huts built out of dough. Two slices of white bread, with the crust peeled off, a couple of tablespoons of Elmer's glue, a few pumps of any kind of hand lotion and you can create all sorts of props.

It is all kneaded together, and then kneaded a bit more on a surface sprinkled with corn starch. It should not be sticky, but silky smooth without any lumps. A drop of food coloring is added to each little ball of dough. A mushroom could have a white stalk with a red cap dotted with white dots. No baking is required but they have to stay dry as they harden. The moss should be sprayed with water to keep it fresh, but the dough pieces have to be taken off while spraying and then returned to their fairy forest. This dough is our favorite for making miniature doll house food, too: miniature pizzas, tiny hamburgers, whole little turkeys on a platter—the sky's the limit.

"Okay, Lester, bedtime," Milo announced as he headed for the stairs. "Good night, son. I'm glad you had a *gut* time."

"Henry, wake up! I can't find Rose," Veronica said as she shook him. "Where can she be? She's never been sleepwalking. I can't find her. I'm sick with worry, Henry."

He stretched and ran his fingers through his hairs. "The outhouse maybe?"

"No, she has the little pot in her room. She knows she shouldn't go out without us," Veronica continued to fret.

"Okay, I'm up. I'll go look," Henry said as he hurriedly dressed. After a full sweep of the house, he headed for the barn, popping his head inside the door of the outhouse on the way. No, she wasn't there either. He went into the barn then and found her sitting cross-legged in the hay in her night gown, cradling her calf, who had almost outgrown her lap by now. She looked up at him and positively beamed.

"She can talk, *Dat!*" she said. He took this in and ran his fingers through his hair once again. What was going on here?

"Watch," she instructed her father. Taking the calf's face in her little hands she addressed it in a tiny voice and asked, "who loves you, *daumling?*"

Right on cue the little lamb said, "*Maaaahhh.*"

"See *Dat,* she thinks I'm her *mamm!*"

"Watch, she'll do it again," Rose said. Addressing the calf once more she asked, "Who do you love most in the whole wide world?"

And again, the calf pronounced an unmistakable, "*maaaahhh.*"

"Well, would ya look at that," Henry played along. No use contradicting her.

"Let's go in and see *Mamm,* huh?" he suggested. "You can show her later, okay?"

"Okay," agreed the little *mamm.*

On their way to the house he asked, "Do you know what day it is?"

"Um..." she thought a moment. "Oh! It's *Grischtdaag!* I almost forgot, *Dat.*"

"Well, we can't forget that" he said.

Rose practically shouted when they came into the kitchen. "*Mamm,* my calf can talk! She can say '*mamm.*'"

Veronica looked at Henry who could only scrunch up his

shoulders and look dumb, but she chose not to contradict him. "Oh, really?" she said. "I see."

"Yes, and she talks to me, *Mamm*. Oh, I am so happy!" she said as she cozied up to the wood stove and rubbed her hands in front of it. Then turning around, she noticed the festive table for the first time. "And it's Christmas!" she noted. "I almost forgot, *Mamm*."

"Wash your hands first and I'll braid you. Then we can have breakfast all together, eh?" Veronica asked.

"Okay," Rose agreed.

"I'll get to the milking and be back real soon," Henry said, heading out the door.

"We'll wait for you," Veronica assured him.

"Now, you, go get dressed and I'll start *mariye-esse*," Veronica told Rose.

"What are you making?" Rose asked.

"You'll see," Veronica replied mysteriously. She didn't have a clue what she would make. She felt more like crawling under the covers again, but that would be out of the question. Not today.

"What am I thinking?" she asked herself aloud. She had completely forgotten she'd made Henry's favorite overnight casserole. She'd thrown it together the day before, wrapped it in foil and put it into the cooler chest on the back steps. It would freeze but would still bake just fine when unwrapped. It was Sausage Hash Brown Casserole, though this time she used the left-over mashed potatoes she had, which turned out just like the original recipe. Sausage, scrambled eggs, plenty of cheese and potatoes made a great fix-ahead meal.

"Whew. And I thought I'd be cooking all day again," she said to herself as she breathed a sigh of relief while filling the coffee percolator with cold water from the spigot on the gravity tank. She set it over the hottest iron plate on the wood stove. It would start to bubble quickly there.

"Just one piece of candy before breakfast," her father warned when they were all seated. Rose quickly picked out a chocolate-covered cherry from the plate before her and popped it into her mouth. Her parents followed suit, also choosing a candy to eat before breakfast, sending Rose into gales of laughter.

"What are we doing today?" Rose asked as cherry syrup trickled down her chin.

"Well, we will get ready for church soon, after breakfast, and when we get back, then we'll get ready for any visitors. We'll fix some snacks and set those out on the table for whoever shows up. We're invited back to Hazel and Eli's for *zapper* at five."

"Can I bring a candy out for my calf after breakfast?" Rose asked.

"By no means, NO!" Milo said emphatically. "That'll make her sick. Really sick."

"But what can I give her for Christmas?" she asked, less hopeful.

"An occasional carrot or apple won't hurt her, but I found her a real treat at the feed store last week. Close your eyes," Milo said as he got up from the table and reached up to the top shelf in the mud room, pulling down a brown bag.

He took out a green pellet, the size of a cookie. "They're alfalfa pellets. They love them and it's a real treat. She'll eat it right outta your hand. Only two a day though, okay? No more than that," he said.

"I'll bring it to her after we eat. Thank you so much," she said, turning over the 'cookie' and then sniffing it.

"Are they *gut* for me too? To eat?" she asked, bringing it to her lips.

Her parents answered in unison: "NO!"

One of the hardest tasks that modern folks face is trying to figure out how to live a simple life.
- Amish saying

CHAPTER 34
Rapple

T he next two days were spent getting ready for their trip to Ontario. The house needed putting back to rights after the busy Christmas Day celebrations. The day after Christmas wasn't any different with families stopping on their way back to their homes to greet everyone whom they didn't see the day before.

The Christmas Chutney was a great success as was the White Christmas pie. Veronica was reading the labels of the numerous little jars lined up on the counter to Rose. Lots of jams and jellies were exchanged as were other small home-made gifts. Quilted hot pads, flour bag towels embroidered in the vintage red-work style, knitted dish rags, and crocheted tea cozies came out of hiding for the holidays after being carefully and lovingly made to give away at Christmas.

"Jalapeno jelly," Veronica read. "I bet that one is hot, ya think?" she asked Rose who scrunched up her nose and shook her head.

"What's this one?" Rose asked pointing to a green one.

"It says 'Tomatillo Salsa.' I think our cousin Grace made it. See, her initials are on the label," Veronica pointed out.

"Oh, look, this quart jar says, 'Soup Supper.' It's all the ingredients to make a pot of soup. See the layers? It looks so pretty." Then opening the envelope stuck to the top of the jar she read aloud to Rose.

"Ingredients: rice, dried black and pinto beans, lentils, split peas—yellow and green—tri-colored pasta or alphabet macaroni, dried onions, parsley and celery, beef flavored bouillon, barley, bay leaf, thyme, basil, and rosemary. It says you can add cooked beef or chicken. The initials say 'JMB.' I bet that's Joe Mildred Beachy. Yes. She's clever like that."

"What's this one?" Rose said moving down the row of jars.

"Rhubarb and strawberry. And that one is marmalade. Then there's peach, strawberry, raspberry, blueberry, blackberry and plum. Blackberry is my favorite," Veronica added.

"Mine too," her shadow agreed. Finally, Veronica sat down at the table with her notepad and pencil.

"We've got to get organized now," she told Rose. "We'll make a list of everything we must do for our trip on Friday. It'll be here before we know it," Veronica said.

"We've got all the presents wrapped in the wood box thingy in your bedroom," Rose remembered, still not privy to the wooden box's origin or purpose.

"Yeah, we'll have to get those all into suitcases. And I want to bring a hamper of food, so we don't have to buy much on the train," she said writing down 'cooler box food' on her list.

"Write down 'Rosemary' too, *Mamm*. We can't forget her. She likes train rides. She told me so," Rose explained.

"Okay. Got it. I wrote that down. We're in pretty good shape. Let's make supper before *Dat kumms* in from chores," Veronica suggested. "We'll put out some of that monkey bread Suzy gave us and the mushroom soup we canned. There's still plenty of desserts to eat up, too."

"Why do they call it 'monkey bread,' *Mamm?*" Rose wanted to know. "I love it. You pull it apart and it's all ooey, gooey, and sweet."

"I think it's called that because you don't slice it like bread, even though you bake it in a loaf pan, but pull it apart and eat it with your hands like a monkey. I guess that makes sense," Veronica reasoned. Rose nodded in agreement.

Henry came into the kitchen and tossed a bundle of mail onto the table.

"There're more Christmas cards in there I'm guessing. I'll slice them open, and you can stack them up. How's that Rose?" he asked.

"Yes!" she answered. "Then we've got to put them up," she explained as he wrestled off his mud-coated boots.

"I don't know where you're gonna do that," her father said. "There isn't an inch left on any of the windows or door frames in this *haus.*"

"We can tack up some grosgrain ribbon over the table, like a banner maybe, nailed up on both ends and pin them onto that," Veronica suggested.

"*Gut* luck with that," Henry said as he hung up his jacket and hat and walked across the kitchen to the chore sink in his stocking feet.

Then there was a knock on the kitchen door. Rose looked up at Henry who was frowning at Veronica. "Who's out now?" he asked, walking back across the kitchen to the door.

"Hi," the boy said in a tiny voice. He held a large cardboard box in front of him. He just stood there.

"Hi, Clarence. *Hallicher Grischtdaag!* What did you bring?" Rose asked. Clarence had proven to be a good friend when Rose had Whooping Cough. Back then he'd brought her a rabbit from his colony at his family farm to keep her company as she recovered.

"Here, let me take that for you," Henry said lifting the box.

Then Veronica said, "Clarence, so *gut* of you to *kumm* over."

"It's for Rose," the child said simply, smiling. "For Christmas."

"Can I open it? Now?" she asked.

"Sure," he answered. Henry put the box down on the floor between the children who immediately started opening it.

"Ohhhh!" Rose said, her eyes tearing up. "*Mamm, Dat,* look at this!" she excitedly told them. "It's a baby *rapple.*"

When they looked into the box, they could also see a darling gray and white dappled rabbit.

"It's to keep Honey Bunny company, see?" Clarence explained as he lifted out the little rabbit and handed it to Rose who sat down cross-legged on the floor and drew it onto her lap.

"Awwww, he's the cutest thing ever! Is it a boy *brunne* or a girl?" she asked.

"I don't know. I can't tell with bunnies," he answered. It didn't really matter much to Rose either way. She was instantly in love with the tiny creature.

"Oh, thank you Clarence. This is the best thing ever. Thank you," she said.

"Clarence, can you stay for *zapper*?" Milo asked.

"No, my *mamm* said I need to get back, but I want to say hi to Honey Bunny before I go if that's okay," Clarence said, before adding, "it's already weaned. It'll eat whatever you give Honey Bunny."

"We can see what they think of each other then," Rose said as she stood up, clutching the little rabbit to her chest.

In the barn Clarence opened the stall where the calf and Honey Bunny lived. Picking up the larger rabbit he exclaimed, "Man, has he grown. He's huge!"

"He eats a lot. Anything we bring him. Do you think this one is a girl? Maybe they can get married," Rose suggested. Veronica and Henry had followed the children into the barn, both amused by the children's innocence.

Rose lowered the little rabbit onto the straw bedding on the floor of the stall. The two rabbits hopped toward each other, faced each other then and sniffed. A minute later they leaned into each other and appeared to go to sleep.

"They'll get along *chust* fine," Clarence pronounced.

"What are we gonna name her?" Rose wondered.

"I donno. You'll think of something. She's yours now," Clarence said, his eyes sparkling. Then he bent down and patted the smaller of the two rabbits and said goodbye.

"Thank you so much, Clarence. *Hallicher Grischtdaag!*" she called as he walked out of the barn.

"*Hallicher Grischtdaag!*" he called back as he skipped down the driveway.

"But who's gonna take care of the bunnies when we go to Canada? *Dat?* Can we take the new one with us, please?" Rose begged.

"You don't have to worry about that. We've already hired the *buwe* next door and they know all about the bunny and your calf, too. They'll be in *gut* hands, Rose," he assured her.

"Besides, Canadian customs won't let you bring it into the country. They're plenty strict about that. One of my cousins wanted to bring his pet hooded rat across the border when they came to visit us once from the states and they had to have papers signed by a veterinarian saying the rat was healthy and had all its shots. Can you believe that? They got the papers and all and then the customs officer didn't even ask about pets when their car pulled up to the Canadian side. My cousin had the papers already to show the man, and his *dat* was *chust* glad it didn't *kumm* up, but they got waved right through. The customs people were more worried if people were bringing in oranges than rats."

"You're kidding," Veronica said.

"No, it's true," Henry chuckled. "And as far as I know we don't have pedigree papers for our rabbits. Case closed." He looked over at a very dejected little girl.

"Listen, Rose. The little one must for sure be happy to have Honey Bunny for a friend. It'll be perfectly happy here. She'd get lonely in Milo's barn if there weren't any other rabbits at night. It'll be much better off here."

"I guess you're right," she said. "And the *buwe* will feed her?"

"Absolutely. Every day. I promise," her *dat* assured her.

"God speaks quietly, very quietly but He does speak, and He will make known to you what He wants you to do."
- C.D.

CHAPTER 35

Forty-Eight Hours

The day after Christmas they loaded up the buggy once more with decorative tins (collected from thrift stores over the preceding months) filled with gingerbread cookies and peanut brittle. They were going to stop in and see two more families that had invited them in the days before Christmas.

"I love Christmas, don't get me wrong, but I can't wait to get to Edith's kitchen and put my feet up and do absolutely nothing," Veronica said in English in a hushed voice as she leaned toward Henry on the buggy bench. The buggy continued bumping and banging along over the potholes and chunks of ice littering the dirt roads.

"I am absolutely done in, Henry," she said, still in English, sighing deeply.

"I can imagine," he answered, also in English. "*Chust* think, ten days in bed with absolutely *nothing* to do but take care of this little one, napping when he does, come January, right?"

"Ooooh. That sounds like heaven. I can't wait," she purred as she rested her head on his strong shoulder. He shifted the rein in his right hand to join the other one in his left and reached around her shoulders to hold her close.

"Well, you better wait, you! No fair coming early. You have a *gut* talk with that one, please," he teased his wife. Well, only half teased. The alternative was unthinkable.

They could hear then a little voice from behind the bench as they bounced along. "*Pennsylfaani, denki,*" it said.

"So, who is it we're visiting today?" Rose wanted to know.

"It's Phoebe and Stephen. I've promised to visit since forever," Veronica told her.

"Do they have any *kinner* I can play with?" Rose asked hopefully.

"As a matter of fact, they do," her *mamm* said. "*Ztzvilling,* actually."

"For real?" Rose bounced up on her knees and wrapped her arms around Veronica's neck from behind where she'd been sitting...with Rosemary tucked under her arm, of course.

"Two boys or two girls?" she asked.

"Neither," Veronica answered.

"But that's all there is," she puzzled.

"No, actually there is one more combination with twins," Veronica said, letting that sink in for a minute.

"No, there is not," Rose said. "Tell me," she demanded.

"Well, their names are Naomi and Matty."

"Oh. Now I get it! A boy *and* a girl," she answered.

"You are correct," her dad solved the mystery.

"How old are they? Like me?" Rose wanted to know.

"They're littler. About three, I'm wagering," Veronica answered.

"Both of them?" Rose asked again.

"Yup. That's how that works, *darr,*" Henry said.

"Oh," Rose said sitting back down and arranging Rosemary's quilt tightly around her.

"So, they can talk?" she asked.

"I am guessing they can," Veronica answered. "I certainly hope so."

"We should get twins," Rose said then. "Wouldn't that be *wunderbar-gut?*"

"Hilarious," Henry answered dryly.

"Where do you get them from anyway, *Mamm?*" she asked, throwing Veronica into a panic. When she relaxed again, she attempted to put this conversation to bed.

"*Gott* decides all that. Now, have you still got the cookies and peanut brittle back there? They aren't sliding all over the place?" Veronica asked.

"Yup, we're all *gut,*" she answered.

They rode on down the lane and turned onto another dirt road heading east this time. It was a beautiful sunny, though crisp morning. They passed several buggies going in the opposite direction, often full of children who waved at them as they rode by. Horses and cows dotted the rolling hills, using their hoofs to push away the snow so they could munch on the grass below.

Children were outside one farm building snow men and at another home the young people were skating up and down a narrow frozen stream. There was a clothesline there with towels and cleaning rags pegged to it. No proper washing would be hanging on the lines today. It was still Christmas.

Rose curled up then in the woolen army blanket on the buggy floor, Rosemary tucked tightly in her arms.

Veronica craned her neck around to see in back.

"I do believe she's napping back there," she commented.

"We were up late, ya know," Henry answered.

"So, what names are you considering?" he asked Veronica.

"Oh, I hadn't really thought about that much. What are your thoughts?"

Henry thought for a minute. "Well, if it's a girl, maybe another flower name. Like Clover, maybe."

She swatted his arm with her mitten at that, laughing out loud. "You're not serious, are you? You are? Clover is a name for a cow, you silly."

"Well, maybe Holly, *kumming* near Christmas, ya think?" he asked.

"Ya, that's *gut*," she agreed. "And a boy?" she asked.

"I donno. What about Christ?" he said, which made her laugh.

"I gotta tell ya," she began, laughing, "but when we were little there was this crabby old guy, an *Englischer* he was. Even the *Englische* children feared him. We all thought he lived in a haunted *haus*. He never cut the grass, and the shutters were falling off the windows. A proper haunted *haus*. On Halloween, the neighborhood kids who were trick-or-treating, not the *Amische kinner*, mind you, would empty a whole can of shaving cream into his mailbox, then shut the door on it and play other tricks on him. Anyway, his name was Christ. I'd always think of him. No, we can't use that name."

"How 'bout Emanuel?" Henry asked.

"Oh, I like that. Ya. Very much," she replied. Then she laughed.

"Now what's so funny?" he asked.

"Your baby *chust* kicked me. He likes the name, too, I think," she explained.

Then they arrived at the Troyer's farm. Stephen came out to greet them and help with the horse. Rose was lifted down from the buggy and stood there blinking at all the whiteness. The snow sparkled. There wasn't a cloud in the sky. She shuffled after her mother who was waddling up to the porch, carrying the cardboard box of goodies as they all made their way to the house. As Rose followed, she saw two little faces, noses smushed into the windowpanes fogging the glass up while watching as their guests arrived.

First, they peeled off their wraps and stamped off the snow on the rug before removing their boots altogether. The twins were bouncing up and down, barely able to contain their utter glee at having a new playmate all to themselves for the day. The second Rose was free from her outer clothes, they raced off to their room, Rose running close behind.

"So how are you?" Phoebe asked as she led their guests into the big kitchen.

"We're gut," Henry answered. "On our way to Canada day after tomorrow," he said.

Phoebe's eyebrows instantly went up. She looked at Veronica, and then down from her eyes to the elephant in the room: a belly that could no longer hide the obvious.

"Really?" Phoebe asked. "Are you serious?"

"Well, I'm not technically due till January," Veronica explained, though it sounded rather lame at this point. "We'll be there in time for *Ztvett Grischtdaag*. See, I can *chust* relax and not do a thing the whole time up there. Then we'll be home in plenty of time. He might not *kumm* until a week or even two later. They often do that, ya know," she reasoned.

"Well, I don't know if I would be that confident," Stephen joined the conversation. "I *chust* hope you have a Plan B."

Henry was listening to all this. "So, as a nurse, you think it's a bad idea?" he addressed Phoebe.

"Well, I can't say for sure. It's close. I'd think seriously first," she answered. "What does your midwife say?"

"She says it might wait till January. He doesn't feel like he is over seven or eight pounds yet. It could still be a few weeks," Veronica explained, hoping to sound reasonable.

"Good luck with that," Phoebe laughed. "Keep us posted, okay?" Getting up from the table then announced, "I'll *chust* check on the *kinner* and then you'll have some snack with us?"

She returned a minute later smiling. "You'd think they've been siblings forever. They're playing so nicely. I'll call them after a bit. Let's let them play," she suggested.

"So, tell me, what's it like being a nurse? Are you kept busy?" Veronica asked.

"You have no idea. I'm on call twenty-four-seven. You can't imagine. Everything from babies with croup, whole families with influenza, questions about Lyme's disease, broken toes, you name it. One *mamm* even sent a buggy to pick me up because her dog was having puppies and it seemed to be taking too long and she was worried," she laughed. "Usually all I can do is suggest they go to Urgent Care if it seems serious, otherwise I'll make an appointment for them with someone in town and ask them to let me know how it goes, if I need to follow up."

"That's for sure handy, though. When you're worried about your *kinner* you really aren't always thinking straight, are you?" Veronica said.

"And there's two now at home, close to Eternity. So happy they can be with their families. Both elderly *gross-mammis*. They're so thankful for the littlest thing you can do for them."

"Well, you were a godsend when Rose had Whooping

Cough. I'll always be grateful for your help, Phoebe," Henry said. "We were *kumming* pretty unglued at that point, for sure."

"Do you still see the other nurses you graduated with? How are they doing?" Veronica wanted to know.

"The Mennonite girl, Leah that married that Amish boy, Ben, was able to adopt a baby. They'd tried close to two years and were pretty broken up about not getting *schwanger*. They are so happy now. I see them from time to time. They've applied to adopt again. They went all the way to Siberia, too, last time."

"Boy, have they got stories about that trip. It's for sure another world over there," Stephen said. Then he added, "maybe we should go there and adopt, ya think? I'd love to see it there."

"No way, José. We'll have this one by Easter. Why would I want to go to Siberia?" Phoebe said, shaking her head.

"But what an adventure," he added.

"Nope. Not happening, Mister," Phoebe ended that discussion. Then she continued.

"The other nurse was on mission work there with her husband and was able to facilitate the whole thing. That's Hilda and Ivan. They're Mennonites. They've since *kumm* back to the U.S. and have two now. And the Hutterite girl is kept very busy. Susanna has a mobile clinic that the county funded, set her up in a mobile unit so she can visit other colonies. They go all over the Midwest. He drives and they bring their little guy with them. The colonies write and ask for them and then she sees anyone who wants to visit with her, answers all their questions. Some of the colonies are so few and far between they don't have doctors in some of those rural areas at all. But then even when they do, not many *fraus* will feel comfortable talking with a male doctor about intimate stuff, much less have him examine them. She can do basic nursing, take blood tests and mail them in to a lab back home and all sorts of things."

Veronica nodded in agreement. "That is sure great. That would really help a lot of people who might otherwise *chust* doctor at home with herbs or supplements."

"You absolutely wouldn't believe what she tells me about some of the old wives' tales out there," Phoebe said shaking her head. She continued. "She said one old woman told her that her mother was told that to cure her daughter's asthma she had to skin a muskrat and lay the hide on the child's chest. Can you believe it?"

The others groaned, frowned and shook their heads.

Then Phoebe added, "I looked it up, too. Muskrats can carry and transmit cysticercosis, tularemia, Tyzzer's disease, and biotoxin poisoning. It's a wonder more *kinner* haven't died being on home remedies."

Phoebe continued. "Salves, poultices, plasters, teas, and tonics—you name it, and they've thought it up. Someone could write a book about alternative Plain remedies. It's not *chust* the Hutterites. They've all got them. I've had *gross-mammis* in our own district tell me that dandelion is a common remedy for a variety of ailments, including diabetes, dropsy, and liver problems. Sometimes I don't know what to tell them."

"That's true. You see all these quacks advertising all sorts of alternatives; they promise they can cure everything from cancer to mental illness, all sorts of nutty things that aren't gonna help at all, and they must spend thousands of dollars, all for nothing in the end," Phoebe explained. They all nodded.

"Did she tell you if ya put it fur side down or skin side down?" Veronica asked, still horrified at the thought of it. "The muskrat hides. It might make a difference." They all shook their heads, snickering.

"She also told me about a woman she met who was standing under a gingko tree, eating the leaves one after another. She told Susanna that they cure *chust* about everything. The tree was almost bare, too," she laughed. "There were still leaves above about six feet from the ground where she couldn't reach," Phoebe added. "*Chust* the top half."

"Did she ask what was wrong with the woman, like, what was she trying to cure?' Veronica asked.

"Ya, she did, actually. The lady told her she was fine. It was *chust* to prevent getting sick," Phoebe explained.

"Yeah, right," Stephen added, incredulously. "Tell me another one," he remarked dryly.

"Say, did any of ya see that ad in *The Budget* this week for a fundraiser called Harmonicas For Hope? It's over in Apple Creek. A whole-day event of harmonicas. Should be pretty cool," Stephen said. "I'm thinking of going to check it out."

"Interesting," Henry said. "I'd like to see that," he added, chuckling.

"One last quickie," Phoebe said she wanted to share. "Have you ever heard of the 'Amish Miracle Cure?' It's supposed to cure hearing loss. Deafness. Really."

"What's in it?" Veronica asked.

"If I remember correctly, it a bunch of antioxidants–gingko is one, that's what made me think of it. Also, B12, magnesium, and zinc."

"Good luck with that," Henry said.

"Well, how 'bout eating now?" Phoebe asked. Again, they all nodded as she jumped up from the table and headed for the pantry, returning with not one but two pies *and* a cake.

"I know it's 'bout dinner time, but we've got so many baked things they've all brought us that we have to use it up somehow," Phoebe explained.

"I have no problem with that," Henry chuckled.

"Me, either," Stephen agreed. "Any of that ice cream still in the freezer outside?" he asked.

"Yup, loads. I had the same thought," Phoebe said as she headed out.

"Well, there you go," Veronica laughed. "That's your protein right there, eh? A perfectly balanced meal."

Then Henry suggested he get the children.

They were playing happily in one of the back bedrooms. A line of plastic and wooden horses was lined up across the center of the room, like a covered wagon convoy trekking West. Against the far wall, a row of faceless Amish dolls of varying sizes were propped up against the base board as if watching it all. The three children were busy standing up tiny plastic farm animals inside a plastic fence in front of a doll house. Pigs, donkeys, chickens, sheep, dogs and goats populated the fenced-in area. Clothes peg people stood frozen upright inside the doll house in the various rooms.

"Dinner is ready, y'all," Henry said. The little animals didn't get to join the others in the paddock but were left on the floor for later as the children got up and ran to the kitchen.

Them that works hard eats hardy.
- (very) old Amish saying

CHAPTER 36
Mechanical Mice

Finally, the day arrived. The little family waited in the front room of their home with their coats and shawls on, watching for the van that would take them to the Amtrak station. Henry looked down at Rose.

"Is Rosemary excited to go to *Onkel* Milo's?" he asked.

"Oh, yes. It's almost *Ztvett Grischtdaag, Dat.* Did ya know?"

"I know," he played along. "What are ya gonna do first?"

"I'm gonna see if their animals talked on *Grischtdaagnacht* and tell them all about my calf," she explained. "Then I'm gonna give 'em all hugs—my cousins. Then I'm gonna see *Aendi,* my old *mamm,* and the baby, Izzy. Then we're gonna give them all the presents we made, right?"

"Sounds like a plan," he agreed as he lifted two of the suitcases. "It's here," he announced.

"I thought you said we are going on a train," Rose questioned, surprised to see a van.

"We are," Henry said. "The van is taking us to the Amtrak station. The train doesn't exactly *kumm* by us."

Rose nodded that she understood, though not really.

209

Finally, they were tucked into the van—more like squeezed—as they all sat between boxes, suitcases, and rucksacks. The ice chest was wedged between the back of the driver's seat and the floor. Rose's feet went on top of it.

"It's like playing sardines," Rose laughed.

"You got that right," Mrs. Dyck said. Rose took that exchange as permission to speak, though she was pushing the boundaries, and she knew it. "Mrs. Dyck, have you been to Ontario?" she asked.

"Absolutely, my dear. One of my favorite cities. You've got to see the CN Tower, the Royal Ontario Museum, Casa Loma and the St. Lawrence Market. There's even a butterfly conservatory. Get your folks to take you to that, okay?" Rose nodded. "Can we, *Mamm?*" she asked.

"May we?" Veronica corrected.

"Maybe?" Rose asked, though less hopeful.

"We'll see," Henry answered.

The train station was buzzing with activity. Rose had never seen so many people in one place at any one time. Not even at horse auctions her *dat* took her along to a couple of times a year. And they were so varied, people from other counties. Even toddlers who spoke foreign languages. This was extraordinary!

"How does that baby not know English, *Mamm?*" she asked after they stood in line behind the little family while waiting to buy their tickets. Veronica listened for a few moments before answering. "She's speaking Spanish," she informed Rose.

"How did she learn that, anyhow, *Mamm?*" Rose wanted to know. "She's only a *bobbel!*"

"Babies grow up hearing what their parents speak and that's how they learn," she explained.

"Huh," was all she said while she took that bit of information in, while staring at the prodigious baby.

Finally, they boarded the train and found their seats. Henry pushed and shoved their luggage until it was all safely stored above them in the racks. It was close to midnight when the train finally pulled out of the station. Then the lights were dimmed in their section.

"Bedtime," Veronica told Rose as she took out her favorite blanket and wrapped her in it, making sure Rosemary was snug inside, too. They had settled her by the window so they would be sitting next to each other and could talk without bothering her. As soon as they were sure she was asleep Veronica took out a thermos of cocoa and poured two cups. They had the whole night ahead of them to catch up talking. If it was in Pennsylvania Dutch, none of the other travelers would be privy to their conversations, either.

"How are you feeling?" Henry asked her.

"Fat. Grouchy. Ya know. But *chust* glad this *bobbel* is waiting this long to arrive," she answered honestly. "After last time I keep trying to tell myself I should be content being in this state for the next year, whatever it takes...."

"I understand," Henry sympathized.

"How could you?" she shot back defensively. "If only *dats* could have *bobbeli*, then you'd understand. And we'd for sure be extinct as a species by now were that the case," she smirked.

"I *chust* meant—" he began.

"I know. Sorry for snapping at you," she regressed. "It's *chust* the most absurd existence, finding yourself transformed into a beached whale, or some kind of enormous manatee. And at least they get to live in water and *chust* float around all day. I get to carry the whole thing, upstairs and down...I can hardly eat, there's no room left even."

He reached around her shoulders and pulled her close. "Well, don't let Junior there hear you. Not *chust* yet," he said, tenderly running his hand over her belly. "We still have a bit over two weeks. You can give him his eviction notice once we're back home, okay?"

"And what if he'd be *chust* like Rose and has a mind of his own? What then?" She remembered the earlier run in she'd had with Rose. "Did you notice her pedicure?" she asked.

"What are you talking about?" he frowned.

"She painted her nails '*chust* like the ladies at the farmers' market' she said. You didn't see them?" she asked.

"No way. Who gave her that idea?" he wanted to know.

"Your daughter thought that one up all on her own," she answered, shaking her head.

"Hmph," was all that came out of him. Then, "here, drink your cocoa before it gets cold."

Just at that moment the lights and the intercom switched on and the conductor announced the next stop, loud and clear, should anyone miss their stop. "TRAVERSE CITY, NEXT STOP. TRAVERSE CITY. THIRY MINUTE STOP. THIRTY MINUTES, FOLKS. TRAVERSE CITY."

"Did she sleep through that?" Veronica asked, sounding rather miffed.

"Didn't budge," Henry reported after looking down at her.

"That's *gut*."

"Is it breakfast time yet?" Henry asked.

"You're hungry already?" Veronica asked incredulously.

"*Chust* bored, I guess. What do we have for breakfast anyway, in that cooler you made up, so I can look forward to it," he asked.

"Blueberry scones, cream cheese, bananas, *kaffi* and hard-boiled eggs," she rattled off the menu. "Does that suit you?" she asked.

"Can't wait," he answered. Then he winked. She leaned back on his shoulder and closed her eyes, suddenly sleepy. He kissed the top of her head and let his head rest on hers.

The next day started around five a.m., later than he usually rose to start the morning milking. It was not quite dawn yet, but Henry had been up, watching the scenery go by. Then suddenly, he started seeing deer, or were they caribou? There were hundreds of them as the train passed through a rocky landscape, devoid of anything else, hardly any trees, just rocky outcrops, layer upon layer of exposed sedimentary rock and boulders, almost like a moonscape. He wiped the window glass with his sleeve and stared out. There were whole herds of whatever they were. And they were all facing the train tracks as if watching the people go by. He nudged Veronica and pointed out the window when she opened her eyes. She blinked and whispered, "Oh, my! What are they?" as if she'd spook them if she spoke above a whisper.

"Big horn sheep or maybe mountain goats I'm thinking. Might be caribou. I don't know. They're traveling south, looking for food. I can't believe it. There're thousands of 'em!" he said, awed by the sight. Slowly the herd thinned out as the train neared a settlement of some sort.

"I bet we're *kumming* into a reservation. The Neskantaga First Nation are on the map about here. It's an Oji-Cree community. There's Attawapiskat Lake. See?" Henry explained.

"I was always fascinated by Native lore," he continued. "I made sure we studied it when I was still teaching. It's amazing. I guess, like us *Amische,* in a way, they have been able to preserve an entire culture while surrounded by a changing world. Plenty of obstacles, though, all the same worldly temptations for the next generations, eh?"

"Well, I'm going to see if I can find the bathroom," Veronica announced. "I'm not sure I'll even fit in there when I do find it..." she said, speaking more to herself than to Henry.

When she returned but before she had a chance to sit down in her seat he asked, "Is it *mariye-esse* time yet?"

"Well, can we wait *chust* until she's up for breakfast and washed up first before we get into the cooler chest maybe?" she asked.

"Ya. That would be better," he agreed.

The rest of the day was filled with story books and Christmas stories Rose had heard many times already but never tired of. Henry had not heard *Brother Heinrich's Christmas* when Veronica read it at Rose's bedtime several nights before, so they read that—twice. It had become one of Rose's favorites.

At lunchtime, the train stopped at a major crossroads where many people got off and met other connecting trains. The conductor announced as they were pulling into the station that they'd have one hour and would leave promptly at twelve thirty.

It felt wonderful to stretch their legs and walk around. They headed down a busy street and did a bit of window shopping. The store windows were elaborately decorated for Christmas, one with a scene of Santa's workshop and dozens of elves helping build the toys. The figures were motorized, and each wielded a sewing needle, a hammer or a paint brush. There were even two mechanical mice skit-tering around the elves' feet and a cat who looked quite real sleeping under a work bench. Rose stared with her mouth open. Even Henry stood there trying to figure out how it was all built and powered. It was duly impressive. They headed back toward the train station then after buying a bag of hot roasted chestnuts from a pushcart vendor by the station.

Back on the train, having enjoyed the fresh air, they assembled their lunch from the offerings in the cooler chest. As they were eating several *Englischers* walked by their seats and remarked, "Boy, you guys were smart. Here the dining car has run out of most of the things on the menu. Plenty of scrambled eggs left, but not much else. You guys are sure lucky!"

After they ate, they were all lulled back to sleep by the rocking train as it sped onward North.

Henry entertained Rose with a game of Uno, which, surprisingly, she seemed to catch on to. After that they played, 'I Spy with My Little Eye' naming something red, or something round or something blue, taking turns 'spying.' When they had exhausted that, Henry pulled out a game he'd saved just for this trip. It was a magnetic set of checkers. He patiently showed Rose the moves and how it all worked. Of course, her pieces hopped all over the place, contrary to the rules, but it was a start. Next, they played Rock Paper Scissors which left Rose rolling in gales of laughter.

After that Veronica twisted and tucked all their handkerchiefs into three mice which you could even make hop and jump. By four o'clock it was almost dusk, and they had run out of ideas to pass the time. They pulled out the cooler chest once more and lined up the paper plates and paper napkins on their laps for supper. More *Englischers* passed them once again on their way down the aisle from the dining car, remarking on their enviable supper there.

"It's like having picnics all day," Rose observed. Then

she said, "Rosemary wants to know if there are any cookies for *zapper?*"

"There *chust* might be, but after your sandwich," Veronica said. Then, correcting herself, she revised that answer. "After *she* eats *her* sandwich."

> *Sitting all day makes one lazy.*
> *- Amish saying*

CHAPTER 37
Amish Yum Yum

It was evening when the taxi drove up to Milo and Edith's farmhouse. Henry and the driver unloaded the suitcases, boxes, cooler chest, and rucksacks onto the porch by the front door.

"Can I ring the doorbell?" Rose asked.

"Go for it," Henry said.

There was no one in sight anywhere on the farm. As the van pulled away from the house, the horses in the paddock turned to watch it drive away before returning to their hay bale sitting up on the pasture feeder. The entire scene was covered in snow. Snowbanks as high as four feet or more were piled on either side of the driveway and along the path from the house to the barn. Three snowmen greeted them from the yard, complete with frozen carrot noses, charcoal eyes and woolly scarves around their necks. There was so much more snow than what the little family had left behind them in the States. The air was crisp but not frigid. Clothes lines were stretched between the porch on the house and a giant maple tree off to the left of the house and rigged up with an elaborate manual pulley system. Rock solid diapers hung the entire length of one of the lines to be brought in later in the day to finish drying on the wires threaded between the beams and the drying racks in the basement *kesselhaus*.

A minute later the door slowly opened. A little boy, maybe four-years old, stood there sizing up the visitors. Without a word, leaving the door ajar, he ran back to where he had come from. Veronica looked at Henry with a tired smile. Rose pushed the doorbell once again, which really wasn't warranted as a whole flock of children came running into the front hall just then, followed by their parents. Everyone was talking at once. The children were jumping up and down and hugging Rose who held Rosemary in a tight grip, managing one-arm hugs in return. Milo pushed his way past the squirming mob to grab a suitcase. Above the din, Edith shouted, "In the house. Now!" as she unsuccessfully tried to steer the ecstatic crowd out of the way.

"You're letting in all the cold air!" she boomed.

The party moved slowly into the house as the two brothers hauled in the luggage that had been piled onto the porch. Finally, with everything and everyone inside, they began hanging up coats and shawls and scarves and pulling off mittens and boots.

"*Kumm*," Edith called to Veronica over the noise. "We're *chust* sitting for *zapper.*" Lester hauled the last suitcase in, pushed the door closed and turned to Milo.

"*Dat*, did you know they were *kumming?*"

"Ya. We did," he answered chuckling.

"Well, ya sure kept that one under wraps, *Dat*," he laughed.

"Help me get some more chairs," Milo asked.

Abby saw what else was needed and set up three more places for their guests. Putting down the silverware she was holding, she turned to Rose and asked, genuinely concerned, "Why are you crying, Rose?"

"'Cause I missed you all so much," she sniffed. "And I'm so happy to be here," she added as she reached out and hugged Abby.

Izzy had been sitting in her highchair the whole time while they'd all abandoned her to greet everyone in the front hall. She bounced in her chair, delighted when they all returned to her in the kitchen.

Rose saw her then and went over to the highchair to greet the baby.

"I missed you, *leibling*," she told her as the baby laughed and waved her arms, energized by all the commotion.

Finally, everyone was seated at the table. Milo cleared his throat, hoping to restore some order.

"*Patties down?*" he began. The kitchen was instantly quiet. That is until he reached for a napkin and broke the spell. But the children didn't talk even then. They didn't say a peep. They knew at the table, and especially with guests present, that children should be seen and not heard. All but the baby, apparently. She squealed with delight and pounded on her tray. Edith reached over to her, stuffing her pudgy hands down under the tray.

"Okay, youse," Edith said to her after the silent prayer as she filled her little plastic Paddington Bear bowl with tidbits from the platters at the table. Immediately upon receiving her supper, Izzy carefully chose one item at a time, popping each in her mouth.

"So how was the trip?" Milo addressed his brother.

"It was looonnng but we made it," Henry answered relaxing into his chair back. "The wildlife was *erschtaunlich*," he said.

"Ya," Milo answered. "The caribou are getting mighty

hungry about now, moving South from the Arctic Circle, all the ones that didn't *kumm* down earlier so far."

"I've never seen so many," Henry added as Edith made up plates for the children which were passed down the line to them.

Edith had outdone herself. It was a feast. She'd known they'd be coming and hoped they wouldn't be too late, waiting for a taxi. The children were so excited by the gifts they'd received for Second Christmas earlier in the day that they hadn't noticed the extra cooking and baking Edith had been up to. The day before she had even managed to make two large White Christmas pies. The table was laden. Amish Yum Yum Salad jiggled in its glass bowl in the center of the table, well, not straight center but as close to it next to the acorn village that the children had been adding to since first constructing it.

There were baskets of potato rolls, made with leftover mashed potatoes, sweet onion cake–though it could be called a bread—apple, butternut and sausage bread stuffing, hearty baked beans simmered overnight in real maple syrup, slow-cooked sauerbraten with spaetzle, and glazed cabbage rolls swimming in tomato sauce, not to mention roast duck and sauerkraut dressing. Dessert would be served later in the evening and must include, for Christmas certainly, all sorts of pies often not seen but once a year.

"Lenny, slow down. We're not in a hurry," his dad said.

Then Edith asked Veronica, "How long can you stay?"

"Well, we are anxious to get home but a couple of days should be okay," she answered. Edith nodded knowingly. She had also prayed that Veronica and the baby be kept safe. It could be thought of as a gamble, travelling in her ninth month like this. But Second Christmas was such a special time. It would only get harder to come together as their families continued to grow in the future.

In the kitchen Milo, Henry, Lester and even Lenny all pitched in on the cleanup. Milo had announced just before the final prayer that since Edith had knocked herself out making their Second Christmas dinner so special, then the men should do all the cleanup and let the *mamms* relax in the living room.

Edith pulled a hassock over to the bentwood hickory rocker for Veronica to put her feet up on once she'd sat down.

"Ohhh, you don't know how *gut* that feels," she said, her eyes closed.

"Uh, yes I do," Edith countered that statement.

"I could only sit upright on the whole train ride. It leaves you achy. A bit swollen, too," she said stretching her arms and wiggling her fingers and her toes. "My, but that dinner was absolutely *abbeditlich,* Edith. You must be done in, eh?"

"Actually, Abby and Ruby are turning into reliable helpers. They can peel, chop, stir and knead if you show them how first. They can run and fetch from the root cellar or the freezer chests out back. They love helping and I love hearing them humming as they work," she explained, smiling at the memory of earlier in the day when she'd enjoyed watching them working together.

"That Yum Yum was yummy," Veronica giggled. "What do you have in it?"

Edith jumped up from her seat and found her recipe box on the kitchen counter. She returned and handed it to Veronica along with a blank card and a pen.

"*Denki,*" Veronica said studying the card before copying it.

Ingredients

- 2 cups water
- 1 (20 oz) can crushed pineapple with juices
- 1/4 cup sugar
- 1 (6 oz) box orange Jello
- 1 (8 oz) package cream cheese, room temperature
- 2 cups heavy cream

Preparation

1. In a medium-sized saucepan, combine water, pineapple (with juices), and sugar and bring to a boil. Continue simmering for 4-5 minutes, whisking often to prevent burning.
2. Take pan off the heat and whisk in Jello until fully dissolved.
3. Chill the Jello mixture for about 30 minutes or until it begins to thicken.
4. In a large bowl, beat cream cheese until smooth, then slowly mix the heavy cream until fully combined.
5. Pour the chilled Jello mixture into the cream mixture and beat until fully blended.
6. Pour mixture into a serving dish if desired, then cover and chill until fully set, about 3-4 hours.

As Edith warmed up their mugs of coffee, Veronica began to copy the recipe.

"This is different from mine. No wonder it's so *gut*," she said.

"I'm not sure if my measurements were off, or what," Veronica said.

Sitting down at the table, Edith sat back and enjoyed her coffee.

"ACH!" Veronica groaned.

"What is it?" Edith jumped in her chair. "Are you okay?" she asked.

"Ugh, I'm fine," she said letting out a long breath. "I probably ate too much. I'll be fine. *Chust* tuckered out," she reasoned as she massaged her belly.

"Close your eyes for a bit. We'll have dessert a little later when they're all done in the kitchen," Edith suggested, watching Veronica closely.

"I think I will take a short nap. You can tell Henry to bring down the suitcase with the gifts when they're done with the dishes. The *kinner* will enjoy that."

Edith got up to talk to Henry about the suitcase, but before she left, she stopped and looked down at Veronica.

"You're not toying with the idea of having this *bobbel* up here, are ya?" she asked.

"No, no. Absolutely not. No way! He's not due for two weeks, at least. He could *kumm* even up to two more weeks after that. No, I'm *chust* tired. Really. Don't worry. I have no intentions of having this *bobbel* anywhere besides my own nice warm cozy bed," she assured her sister-in-law.

There are many black cows but they all give white milk.
- Amish saying

CHAPTER 38

Zwett Grischtdaag

As they were finishing up the supper dishes, Milo looked up from the sink and announced, "Well, it seems we did get that blizzard they were predicting. Would you look at that. It's almost a white-out. I better get the rope out for the way to the barn tomorrow. People could get lost only twenty feet from home in this." Lenny piped up then,

"We can make more snowmen tomorrow with Rose, can't we *Dat?*"

"Sure thing. She'd like that I bet," he answered pouring the dishpan water down the drain finally where it would travel next to the kitchen garden. The pipe had frozen earlier that week, and they had to pour boiling water down the drain in the kitchen and along the PVC pipe outside.

The gifts were the icing on the cake that day. Everyone admired all the hard work that went into making the beautiful things that were exchanged. Milo and Edith's children had also been busy making gifts for Rose. Lester built a doll-size cradle for Rosemary. It was a work of art, considering he had only just turned ten. His father helped him, of course, but Lester had learned so much making it, how to cut and assemble not only basic dovetail joints but also double dovetails. Without access to power tools, it was an arduous job done by hand requiring exact measurements and much time and patience. There was also a new doll-size quilt from Abby for Ruby. It was a nine-patch pattern and Abby was quick to tell her that it's the same pattern Laura and Mary learned to sew first in the Little House books.

Her own parents were able to hide Rose's gifts while filling the suitcases and brought along a new pair of skates. She had grown so fast that when they tried to lace up her old pair from only last year, as soon as the ice rink was ready last month, they couldn't even get them on her feet, which prefaced plenty of tears and then reassurances that they'd find a new pair for her, maybe at a thrift store. Nothing had materialized in that department before this trip.

Edith managed to knit Rose skating socks, what with all her spare time, (of course) and Milo ordered a new Chinese Checkers game for Rose, their old one missing whole groups of marbles over the years, even though she had enjoyed playing it while she still lived with them, back before Veronica met her dad. He had actually ordered two sets, thinking it was time to replace their old one and to give his brother's family a new one, too.

Milo loved the fishing lures Henry made for him, and Edith couldn't believe that Veronica had managed to sew pajamas for all six of her children and a lovely muslin night dress for herself.

After the wrapping paper had been collected and twisted into kindling sticks, and the room put back to rights, they had dessert, though it was later than they were ever allowed to stay up. It was Second Christmas.

Put the swing where the children want it. The grass will grow back.
~ From an Amish cookbook

CHAPTER 39

Blizzard Babies

As the dessert was shared around the table, Veronica stood up from her chair and excused herself. "I'm gonna go lie down again. Please excuse me. I'm tired. I'm sorry," she said, involuntarily rubbing her stomach. She hobbled to the door to the outhouse behind the kitchen, grabbing the flashlight hanging on the portal. Making her way out the door she was suddenly wracked with another pain and bent in half standing there in the snow, gasping. *It's chust those practice ones, what are they called? Brackston-Hickson something or other,* she told herself. It abated within seconds. "See," she told herself aloud. "The real thing is much worse than that."

Finally, tucked into bed in the guest room she instantly fell asleep. All around her the rest were preparing for bed, too, as the snowstorm raged on. Only ten minutes later Henry came into the guest room and quietly undressed, and wearing only his thermals, slipped under the covers. He snuggled up to her back to warm himself. The temperature had already started dipping into the minus numbers, -28.89 Celsius to be exact, or minus 20 degrees Fahrenheit.

Edith cleaned up the whole downstairs and kitchen before calling it a day. In bed finally, too wound up to sleep, she whispered, "Hey. You still up?"

"Ya," Milo answered drowsily.

"I'm worried about Veronica," she said.

"She's not due for two more weeks or even more than that she told you, right?" he asked, turning toward her and propping himself up on an elbow.

"I know, but you remember our Ruby came *three* weeks early. I don't think they ever know exactly. And she was nine and a half pounds, too," she remembered.

"Well, you might have to catch up on your midwifery skills," he chuckled.

"Don't you tease me. The only births I've ever been to are my own," she said in all seriousness.

"Well, you were at that lambing, the one with triplets, even, remember?" he continued.

"*Beheef dich!* I didn't do a darn thing," she shot back.

"No, really? What would we do?"

"Well, I don't know. I suppose call a driver and get to the hospital, eh?" he said, thinking he'd solved the problem.

"No, not in this storm you wouldn't, Mister. Really. *Dunner uns Gewidder!*" she said, though she would have liked to say worse.

"*Chust* go to sleep. We won't solve anything talking all night about it. Nothing will happen. Trust me," he said, hoping it would appease her. Then hoping he was right. Nothing would happen. But what if it did?

Henry turned over in bed. "Can't ya sleep?" he asked.

"I *chust* can't get comfortable," Veronica whined. "I'm going to go down and make a cup of tea. Maybe that'll help. I'm not sure if something at *zapper* didn't agree with me."

"Why, do you feel sick?" he asked, becoming increasingly concerned.

"No. Oh, I don't know. I *chust* don't feel great," she replied. "Go back to sleep. I'll be back soon." And with that she grabbed a flashlight from the bedside table and trudged down the stairs to the kitchen.

Hmmm, she thought to herself when she got down there and found the cupboard with the teas in it. *Hm,* she read the boxes there. *Ethiopian Licorice, Ginger Green Tea, Sleepy Time Tea, Mango Zinger, Hibiscus, I Love Lemon. Ahhh, too many to choose from,* she decided, closing the cupboard. She wandered over to the pantry. There were several Tupperware Pie Keepers there with all the leftovers from lunch and supper. Wandering back to the kitchen table she found the fork caddy and took one back into the pantry with a dessert plate she found by the sink. She opened two of the pie keepers and carefully lifted out a piece from each, closing them and then checking if she'd left any crumbs on the counter there. "Good," she whispered. "Nothing there for the mice." Carefully cradling the snack on the plate, she quietly made her way to the back door off the kitchen and looked out the window.

The snowstorm was raging. Trees were swaying with the terrific winds and debris was flying across the back field. Veronica took a bite of the coconut cream pie as she watched the storm. She shivered then, grateful for being in a cozy house with people she loved. She took a bite next of the chocolate peanut butter pie, chewing it slowly and savoring it as she watched the clothes lines swinging around and around like jump ropes at a game of Double Dutch.

Finishing her snack, she thought she'd try sleeping, or at

least just resting. She could always sleep in late tomorrow. No one would mind. Henry could watch Rose and visit with the rest of the family. Back in bed she listened to the storm whipping a shutter back and forth somewhere on the house. The wind kept up like that forever. She finally fell into a fitful sleep.

Waking up suddenly sometime later she realized it must be morning. She could hear the children's shrill voices above the wind. It was still snowing. She got up and pulled back the curtains on the window and watched the storm. *I'd sure not like to have to go out in this,* she told herself. Before she could take another breath, she was wracked with pain around her middle. She stood frozen by the window, grabbing the sill to steady herself. Biting her lip, she groaned until it abated. "Silly 'practice' contractions," she said to herself. *Better get dressed. Some kaffi might help,* she thought but before she could lift the dress from the peg behind the bedroom door another contraction suddenly rendered her immobile once again. This one took her breath away. With her hands against the wall, she leaned forward hoping she could somehow shake the pain off. It finally weakened enough that she could stand up straight again. *This is ferhoodled,* she told herself. *Not now. Not here. Please, Gott. Not today. It's too early, right?* As she stood there, she tried to decide what she should do next. She grabbed her woolen shawl from a peg and wrapped it around herself. *Chust breathe slowly,* she told herself. She closed her eyes and began inhaling a long breath when suddenly it felt like she'd just been hit by a train. *Oh, help!* she thought. *Just stop. Please Gott, help!*

Just at that moment Henry opened the door and came into the room with a big smile on his face while balancing a tray and pushing the door with his foot.

"Good m—" was all he said until he saw Veronica by the window. "What's wrong?" he asked. It was clear something was up. She continued trying to breathe slowly when another contraction forced her to bend in half while grabbing the windowsill and gritting her teeth. "ARGH!" was all she managed to say. Henry practically tossed the tray onto the bed as he ran across the room to her.

"It isn't really starting, is it? It c-can't be, c-can it?" he stuttered.

She was able to stand up again a moment later. Taking a deep breath she said, "I think it is. I thought it was just practice contractions at first," she said. "I was hoping it was them."

"Oh, like Braxton-Hicks? Is it that?" he asked, panic in his voice.

"No, I think this is really it, I—" was all she could say before she again was having to deal with the increasing all-encompassing pain.

"What do we do?" Henry asked, feeling utterly helpless and fearful.

"I don't know," she replied. "Maybe get Edith."

"Okay. You stay here," he said as he ran out the door and bounded down the steps two at a time.

Right, as if I could go anywhere, she thought riley to herself. Then she laughed out loud. *So bobbeli kumm when they're ready, eh? So, you think yer ready? That's it? Your mamm isn't too happy with you chust now, I'll have you know. Schlechdi! Or boy, or whatever you are. You are naughty.* And with that, another contraction started building.

Henry ran up the stairs right behind Edith who had hitched up her skirts so she could run faster.

"Zum mordsackerment! You think this is funny, eh? There's no way we'll be able to get you to a hospital in this storm.

What were ya thinking?" Then calming down ever so slightly she explained, "I've sent Milo to the phone box in the barn to call an ambulance. I haven't a clue how to deliver a *bobbel*. They better get here in time, I'm telling ya. That's all I'm sayin'...." She realized then that Veronica was dealing with another contraction, trying with all her might to stay focused and probably didn't hear a word she had said. Veronica understood that panicking wasn't going to help alleviate the pain. No way. This was the real thing. Since the beginning of time women have endured this pain. None have escaped it. She wouldn't either. If they had all done it, maybe she could, too. When that one had passed, she looked at Edith.

"I really thought he'd wait, I'm so sorry. He could have even been late, and we'd be back home in plenty of time. I'm thinking you better get a shower curtain or something to cover the bed. I don't want to ruin your mattress when the waters break." As if right on cue, Veronica looked down at her feet to watch the puddle there growing by the second. "Oh, dear!" was all she managed to say. She looked at Edith then. "I'm so sorry. I really am."

Milo made it to the barn following the rope he'd secured there earlier. He knew you could get lost in a white-out blizzard like this. He wouldn't be the first person to freeze to death. Farmers had even burrowed into hay mounds hoping to outlast the driving winds and plummeting temperatures during storms like this, only to be found frozen there after it abated. Some were found only yards from their barns, getting turned around and thinking they'd wandered out to the lower forty.

The Amish district had agreed to place phones

throughout the area to use in emergencies or for business purposes only. They were not in homes because it was decided that chatting on the phone to friends and relatives took one away from the family, much like other modern technological inventions would aid in slowly eroding the lifestyle and values of the Church.

"Operator," the person on the other end announced.

"Um, we need an ambulance as fast as possible," Milo began.

"Your address please..." the operator requested.

"My sister-in-law is in labor. They were up here visiting from the States," he explained.

"I need your address, sir," she insisted.

"Oh, okay. It's 26399 Highway 47 North West," he gave it to her.

"But I don't know how they'll even find the place—" he worried.

"We'll do our best, but the area is experiencing a severe major storm, sir," she explained the obvious.

"I know, but we weren't prepared for this," he said.

"I am notifying the Blizzard Babies* protocol as we speak, sir," she informed him.

"Huh?" Milo asked.

"We send a plow ahead of the ambulance to clear the way, pick up the patient, and then the plow leads the way to the hospital," she explained. "If there's a midwife who has previously signed on to the program in the area, and volunteered to ride with the ambulance, they'll pick her up and she'll come, too. We've got the alerts going out now, sir," she concluded.

"Oh. Really? That's *gut*," he said. "Please hurry!" he added as he hung up the phone and headed back to the house, feeling his way along the rope once again.

"What did they say?" Edith asked as he came into the mud room stomping off his boots.

"They're on the way. She said they'll send a plow ahead of the ambulance to clear the roads," he repeated what he'd just been told.

"I *chust* hope they make it," Edith said, shaking her head before heading for the stairs.

She had prepared the bed and helped make Veronica comfortable. Veronica continued trying to relax and breathe slowly. Henry was sitting next to the bed holding her hand, though he wondered if she might permanently damage it during a contraction when she squeezed so hard and dug her fingernails into his palm.

"OOF! Never again," Veronica announced after the latest contraction died down. "You can have any future babies we have. Have all you want. I am done. No more babies," she said. "You have no idea."

Henry looked over at Edith as she stood across from him at the bedside, his eyebrows imploring a response from her. Anything.

"I always said that too when I had mine," she told Veronica. "And then, the second he's born you forget what you *chust* went through and then you're holding that *bobbel* in your arms. It's a miracle...it's pure magic," she said. Veronica didn't hear a word of what her sister-in-law just said. She was concentrating on another contraction, again paralyzing Henry's hand.

"Where are they?" Edith said. "I sure hope you gave them our address. Did ya?"

"Yes. They didn't say how long they'd take to get here, though," Milo answered.

"Well, whether they make it or not, we need to get ready here," Edith said. "I guess we'll need towels and hot water."

"What's that for?" Milo asked.

"I think to wash our hands and towels to wrap the *bobbel* in. Maybe crank up the stove downstairs so it's warmer up here. It's a bit chilly." she added. Milo obediently dashed out of the bedroom door.

"You doing okay there?" Edith asked Henry.

"No, um, we aren't ready for this, really," he hedged.

"I don't think you ever are. We'll *chust* keep praying and hoping they get here soon," Edith said. As another contraction passed, Veronica looked up at Edith.

"Let's *chust* not do this today. Maybe tomorrow, eh?" Veronica half joked.

"Yeah, right," Edith agreed. "Ya know, Veronica, I'm thinking, women have been doing this since forever, and not always with help. I reckon babies get born anyway, without a whole lot of doctoring. My midwife once told me that your body knows what to do. Instinct. She said even if you'd be in an accident and you're knocked out, your baby will still figure it out."

"You believe that, eh?" Veronica asked. "UuuggggGHH-HHRRR!" she groaned and then practically roared as she felt another rush gaining traction. Her midwife didn't call them 'contractions.' She called them 'rushes' or 'waves' like in the ocean and instructed you to ride over each one. Less medical. A more peaceful idea perhaps?

"You'd better get up on the bed and get comfortable, I'm thinking," Edith suggested. Henry helped her, putting pillows behind her back as Edith directed him where to place them.

Then Edith left the room to find Milo. He was in the kitchen heating the water. He'd found a stack of towels and some soap and had it sitting on the table.

"Here, give me those," Edith said. "I'm thinking she won't want *you* to be there so you should stay down here and keep the *kinner* downstairs, so they don't wander in on us. Feed them something, then go make snowmen or something."

"*Gut* idea. You gonna be okay?" he asked.

"No, I'm *not* gonna be okay," Edith groused. "I'm furious that they came up here when she knew she was this close. And I'm angry with myself for not calling and checking with her before they set out. And I'm scared to death something could go wrong before the ambulance gets here. I haven't stopped praying, and you better not either, stop praying, I mean. We're gonna need a miracle, Milo."

"I know. But *bobbeli* get born in India and Africa and China without doctors..." he began to try to placate her.

"Yeah, and do you know how many babies don't make it in those places? Not to mention the maternal mortality rates, too?" she railed on. "Oh, Milo, I'm scared," she said, bursting into tears.

Milo went over to her and hugged her. Edith honked into her handkerchief and wiped at her eyes.

"We gotta get to work here. No time for *schmuzzling,*" she said, all business now. She hauled the stack of towels toward the stairs as Milo found two hot pads, lifted the canning kettle, filled with hot water and followed her up. She called when she got to the bedroom door. Henry heard and opened it. He had been lining up more mantle lamps on the dresser and bedside tables to provide more light.

"Any sign of the plow yet?" he asked.

"Nothing. It's *chust* us and *Gott* now, I'm afraid," she replied. Veronica had heard that.

"But how will I know when it's time to push?" she asked, quite agitated by the thought of not getting it right somehow. "I don't have any idea what I should do...." she fretted.

"Okay," Edith said taking charge once more. "You don't have to have someone *tell* you when to push. Trust me on this one. When it's time, you'll push and nothing and nobody will be able to stop you then."

"Really? How does that work?" Veronica said, totally unconvinced by Edith's answer.

"*Chust* wait. Now here, sip some juice and try to breathe slowly. When the next rush comes on, *chust* relax and keep breathing really slow. Okay? It's starting up now?" she asked.

Veronica nodded her head ever so slightly, took a deep breath, and tried her best to let it out slowly, calmly.

"That was *gut*," Edith praised her. "Now, I think we should get a sheet over you and get rid of this big quilt," Edith fussed.

"Okay," Veronica agreed. She closed her eyes then, glad for a few seconds worth of relief.

"I have to go to the bathroom," Veronica suddenly announced.

"That feeling happens as the baby's head is *kumming* down. You're close. *Chust* relax. See," Edith encouraged her, "your body knows what to do," she assured her.

"No, it doesn't. If it did it wouldn't have made such a mess of things with my first *bobbel*," Veronica insisted gripping the sheet in both hands.

Edith walked around the side of the bed to where Henry was. She showed him how to keep his wife cool with a washcloth and pinned back her *schtruvvels*.

"How long is this *gonna* be do ya think?" she fumed. "How come they aren't here yet? Hasn't the snow let up at all?" Veronica complained.

Henry answered, "No clue, no and no," he attempted to lighten the mood a bit, were that at all possible. "Cows and ewes and horses take their time, too," he pointed out. "Then the *bobbel kumms* and it's all over with."

"Here's another one." She glared at him as she breathed in once again.

"I'm gonna push!" she suddenly shouted, scaring even herself.

"Are ya sure?" Henry asked, unconvinced. This didn't sound like his wife at all.

She didn't even stop to answer him but took another deep breath and bowing her chin down toward her chest, started pushing. When the rush was over, Edith suddenly remembered what this stage felt like with each of her own children and directed Veronica to stop pushing and rest and only push when the next rush came on. "You are doing so well, honey," Edith encouraged her. Henry didn't know what to do next, so he kept rubbing the cool cloth back and forth across her forehead until she reached up and grabbing it, threw it across the room with all her might. Suddenly she was pushing again.

"That's it," Edith coached her. "Perfect. Now rest a minute." Then Edith lifted a corner of the sheet to see if anything was really going on down there. She was shocked to see a three-inch circle of the baby's head crowning from the birth canal. "Oh...My...*Gott*...Veronica! You are doing this! I can see the head, and it's full of dark curls. Oh! I don't believe this...."

And with that Veronica pushed her baby out who landed on the bed with a plop and promptly howled his disapproval of this new environment he found himself in, being ejected from his snug, cozy home. Henry couldn't stand it anymore and ran around to the end of the bed where Edith had folded back the sheet and threw a dry towel over him. Then she wrapped the baby up with another towel.

"We don't have to cut the cord right away. They say you can wait till it stops pulsing, so the baby gets the rest of the blood from the placenta. Here, my dear, is your *bobbel,*"

Edith said as she handed the crying baby to Veronica, carefully directing the cord along with the baby.

"Is he okay?" Henry asked, worried that there might be something they didn't know they should be doing.

"Those pair of lungs are your answer, Mister," Edith laughed. "There's nothing wrong with *that* one for certain."

"What time was he born?" Edith added.

"Uh, we could say nine a.m." Henry suggested, looking up at the clock on the bedroom wall.

Then Veronica took a deep breath again and said, "It's feeling funny down there."

Edith explained that the placenta usually comes out shortly after and sure enough she was ready with another towel to catch it. She tied the cord in two places with strips she had torn from a clean handkerchief she'd found earlier on the dresser. Then she cut the cord.

It was as if the entire universe suddenly stood still. Nothing else mattered. Here was the most amazing miracle in all the cosmos and they were allowed to witness it.

Edith slowly started tidying up the room and rolling up the laundry. She got a clean nightie for Veronica and checked her stomach as she remembered the nurses always did for her after her babies came. She was satisfied that the uterus was nice and firm where it should be. Veronica handed the baby to Henry then. He could only keep shaking his head. He bent down and kissed his baby several times.

"You really did it, didn't you?" Henry asked, wiping away the tears on his cheeks.

"*We* did it, you silly. I couldn't have done it without you two," Veronica said, chuckling.

Edith asked, "So what are ya gonna name him?"

"We like Emmanuel, being at *Grischtdaag*, and all ya know," Henry said.

Veronica agreed. "He doesn't look like anything yet though. I guess it grows on ya."

Then Henry suggested, "We could call him 'Manuel' or 'Manny' for short."

Then there was a tentative tapping at the bedroom door. Edith went to answer it. She opened it only a crack to check who was there. Milo asked, "How are things here? Me and Rose wanna know."

With her hand still firmly on the door, Edith turned back to scan the room, making sure it was tidy enough for Rose, that there weren't sheets or towels still on the floor. Deciding the coast was clear she opened the door the rest of the way. Rose, still in her nightie ran to Veronica.

"*Kumm* closer," Veronica urged her. "See what I've got," she said brushing back the towel so she could see the baby's face and arms. Rose was speechless. She hesitantly stretched out her hand and stroked the little fuzzy head. "Is it ours?" she asked to which Veronica nodded. "Where did it *kumm* from?" she wanted to know. "The angels brought him last night. Isn't he *wunderbar?*" Veronica asked. Rose was so overcome she started to cry. "And he's really ours to keep?" Again, Veronica nodded her head. Then Rose explained, "I told *Gott* I wanted a *bobbel* so bad."

"Well, I guess He answered your prayers, *liebling*, eh?" Veronica asked. Rose nodded, wiping her tears with her sleeve.

Prepare an inn every day, for the Child to be born in, the Child who was denied an inn in reality, and who still is denied the inns of many hearts.
~ C. D.

* Blizzard Babies was created in the 1980s in several areas of the Midwestern U.S. and was available to any woman in labor who would otherwise not have access to a hospital during a storm. The author was registered with the program as a licensed midwife in rural Wisconsin in the 1990s.

CHAPTER 40
Three Men In A Tub

J ust then there was a loud knocking on the downstairs door. Henry looked at Milo. "Who'd that be?" he frowned.

"I'll go see," Milo said racing out the bedroom door. There was a louder banging once again before he even got to the front door. Flinging the door open he found three paramedics standing there, their arms full of medical bags and equipment.

Milo chuckled, shaking his head. "Well, you guys are about an hour too late."

"The baby's okay?" the first one asked anxiously.

"How is the mother? Is she bleeding at all?" asked the second one nervously.

"The baby breathing okay?" the third one pushed on, obviously extremely concerned.

Milo chuckled again. "Well, everyone's *gut*. He's a good strong baby," he said as he noticed the ambulance then, right behind them in the driveway and the snowplow behind that, both with their lights strobing away. Just then Henry joined Milo in the doorway.

Then the first paramedic said, "We can bring them into the hospital now to get checked out. Can we start then?"

Milo looked at Henry. Then he said, "Well, I don't think that's necessary. We're fine here."

Then the second one spoke up again. "But you might miss something, and we want to do the PKU test in the hospital and then they've got the vitamin K shot for the baby and the erythromycin eye ointment and all. You don't want to miss that. And they can observe him for the first day."

Then the third one spoke, "And they've got to check if your wife has any tears that needs stitching."

"We know what's available, but we aren't interested," Henry dryly informed the three men, his hand already on the doorknob. Then the second man tried harder to convince him adding, "but they can circumcise him while they're in the hospital."

Henry went to close the door then, but not before the first man, who appeared to be their superior stuck his enormous boot in to block the door and said, "Well, okay then. But look, we're required to write a report, so we do need to check everyone out before we leave. May we come in?"

"I guess so," Henry conceded and opened the door all the way. "We're upstairs. Would y'all take off your boots though?" They complied and putting the equipment down removed their boots. Then Henry led the way.

He tapped at the bedroom door and stuck his head in. "Everyone decent? The paramedics are here and need to see that everyone is fine." Veronica looked at and Edith nodded. Edith looked back at Henry and nodded, too.

The three quietly walked in, looking around and taking in the now-tidy room, the soft glow of the lamps and the mother and baby and big sister on the bed.

"Hello, ma'am. We need to make sure you're all okay.

How are you doing?" he asked. The second man took up his clipboard and began taking notes.

Veronica answered, "Ya, we're good."

"And when was he born?" the third one asked.

"At nine," Edith said.

"And it's a boy?" Clipboard Man asked. They all nodded. Thus, they continued asking the questions listed on their forms.

"Well, can I check the baby quickly?" the superior nervously requested. His name tag said 'William SPO.' Veronica nodded, placing the baby all rolled up in towels on the bed. Clipboard Man, whose name tag said, 'Juan MPO' produced a bottle of hand sanitizer for William SPO to use first. Then William SPO slipped on a pair of sterile gloves before he gently unrolled the baby there. Rose was furiously frowning at the proceedings. She leaned over to Veronica then and whispered behind her hand into her ear, "*vorza-ehle?*" Veronica whispered back, "It's okay. They are like doctors, and they want to make sure he's okay."

Then Rose responded, again behind her hand, into Veronica's ear. "I don't want them touching our *bobbel!*"

"They'll go soon," Veronica assured her, pulling her into a hug.

Supervisor William SPO brushed the bottom of the baby's feet one at a time with a finger and nodded to Clipboard Man Juan MPO. He had the baby's chest against his giant palm and looked at the baby's back and nodded again to the other one who checked off another box on the form. Then he rolled the baby over and proceeded to wrap it up before handing the bundle to Veronica. Back safely in Veronica's arms, Rose wrapped her arms around 'her' baby protectively.

"Well, she's really good. Super. You were right," Supervisor William SPO stated, to which paramedic number three, whose name tag read, 'Jack EMS,' officially pronounced to William SPO, "Apgar at forty minutes, ten and ten."

Henry frowned, puzzling. Finally, he asked, "You said 'she'?" Edith, Milo, Veronica and Rose all frowned in unison while looking at him.

"Yes," William SPO responded. "You have a beautiful little girl."

Veronica looked at Edith. "You said it was a boy."

Edith shook her head. "I don't remember saying anything. I *chust* wanted to wrap him up right away cause the room felt coolish."

Henry asked, "Didn't you look, Veronica?"

She answered, "No, I was still in shock I think—"

Rose crawled up on the bed then and carefully unwrapped her 'very own baby' as she was now referring to him—or her. She peeled off the towel and stroked the baby's tummy before leaning over to plant a kiss on her face.

"It's a girl," she uttered, matter-of-factly, and nodded her head once.

The whole room erupted with laughter then. They'd all gotten it wrong. Clipboard Man Juan MPO crossed out what he'd written on his form earlier and wrote 'female,' initialing the revised entry before packing up his clipboard and other equipment in his backpack. He slung it over his shoulder and followed the others.

With that the men left to go downstairs and put on their boots. They all shook hands with Henry at the door and congratulated him on the safe arrival of his new baby *girl*.

As they lined up and left the bedroom one by one, Veronica could hear Rose mumbling under her breath a line from her book of nursery rhymes: "The butcher, the baker, the candlestick maker," very glad to see the backs of them.

"I don't like them touching our baby," Rose said, again informing her parents.

"They've gone, Rose. They aren't bad men. They probably all have their own *kinner* at home," Henry added.

"For sure?" Rose asked to which Henry nodded in the affirmative. Edith was busy rewrapping the baby in a proper little flannel blanket.

"Make her a little burrito," Rose requested. Edith complied and handed the sleeping baby to Rose who was sitting cross-legged in the middle of the bed next to her mother.

"What are we gonna name her?" Rose asked, looking up. Henry and Veronica exchanged glances. Henry winked at her. Veronica only rolled her eyes in response. Then he spoke.

"We kind of like Holly or Heather?" he asked, questioning. "Sorta in line with Rose, eh?"

Veronica answered, "I'm not crazy about either, really. Anything else?"

Edith turned toward the bed. "Would you want to name her after your first *bobbel*, then? Marta?" They turned that one over in their minds for a few moments. Then Veronica answered.

"Nah. Not really. I don't think so. But I can't think of anything else. Can you, honey?"

Henry shook his head. "I can't either," he said as he sat down on the bed.

Then Edith spoke. "I can hear the *kinner* downstairs. We'd better get some *mariye-esse* rustled up. Wanna help me,

Rose?" Rose shook her head 'no' emphatically and hugged her very own burrito tighter.

"I'm starving!" Veronica said.

"I bet you are after all that work. Pancakes okay?" Edith asked.

Rose answered for her *mamm*. "Ya, *denki*."

Henry was on his side of the bed stretched out now with his eyes closed.

"Your *dat* worked hard too," Edith said, laughing as she headed for the stairs going down to the kitchen. He was already sound asleep, snoring softly.

"What will we name her, *Mamm?*" Rose asked.

"I really don't know," Veronica answered her. "How about Ruth or Rachel or Hannah? Or maybe Rebecca or Mattie?"

"Nah," Rose summarily dispensed with those suggestions.

Veronica closed her eyes, too. She hadn't slept a wink all night.

Suddenly, Rose sat up taller. The baby startled for a second but then went back to sleep in her lap.

"We'll name her Merry 'cause she was born on Christmas. Merry Christmas!" she repeated. "Like my best friend Mary."

Veronica opened one eye and looked down on them. "What did you say?" she asked sleepily.

"We're gonna name her Merry Christmas, *Mamm!*" Rose stated.

"Huh. That is kinda cute. Well, let's ask *Dat*," Veronica said closing her eyes once again.

Just then Edith came into the room with a tray piled high with pancakes and coffee, accompanied with all the good things you can put on top of them.

"Wake up, *Dat*," Rose said slapping his knees as he lay there next to her.

"Huh? What?" he grumbled as he opened his eyes.

"Breakfast, *Dat*," she said.

He slowly sat up and helped Edith fill the plates for the three of them.

"I'll eat with the *kinner* downstairs if you don't need anything else here, then," Edith said heading back toward the stairs.

"Here, put her down next to me Rose so you can eat," Veronica told her.

"*Dat!* She's got a name!" Rose practically shouted. Edith turned around in the doorway and froze in place.

"Really?" he asked looking at Veronica, who nodded and said, "Let's say grace first. I'm starving."

The second Henry looked up after the prayer Veronica said, "Rose, you tell him. You thought it up."

Rose made sure she had her *dat's* attention. Then she said, "Her name is Merry Christmas! Do you like it, *Dat?*"

Henry looked back at Veronica who nodded, her mouth already full of pancakes.

"Well, well. Really? Ya both like it then?" he asked, dubiously.

Rose answered, "Ya, and so does Merry. She told me, *Dat*."

Veronica snorted into her coffee at that and scrambled to find a napkin on the tray.

Then *Dat* got his silly look on his face and declared, "Well, then. I guess it is Merry Christmas!"

"In English," Rose pronounced.

Hallicher Grischtdaag to all,
and to all a gut nacht!

248

Don't miss out on your next favorite book!

Join the Satin Romance mailing list
www.satinromance.com/mail.html

THANK YOU FOR READING

Did you enjoy this book?

We invite you to leave a review at the website of your choice, such as Goodreads, Amazon, Barnes & Noble, etc.

DID YOU KNOW THAT LEAVING A REVIEW...

- Helps other readers find books they may enjoy.
- Gives you a chance to let your voice be heard.
- Gives authors recognition for their hard work.
- Doesn't have to be long. A sentence or two about why you liked the book will do.

Afterword

There are at least five people named Merry Christmas that live in Alabama. Small pockets of the Christmas family can be found in Alabama, with others sprinkled around Georgia and Florida. They are probably all descendants of a family originating in England. The name "Christemass" dates to the 1100s and "Christmas" is documented as a surname back to 1492 in England, although its origins are unclear. Some researchers think it was bestowed on people born at Christmas, but others scoff at the claim.

Acknowledgments

I have given birth to a series of books full of true stories and memories gathered from a lifetime of amazing encounters with other cultures and diverse peoples.

I owe a great debt to the mothers and babies I have had the privilege of serving for so many years and all I learned from each one: Amish *mamms*, Hutterite *mutters*, Hmong *nias*, Vietnamese *mẹ*, Somali *hooyo*, Ethiopian *enet*, Native American *shimá,* and all the other brave women I have met.

I also owe a great debt of gratitude to WOW (Women of Words) and NLW/RWA (Northern Lights Writers/ Minnesota chapter of Romance Writers of America) and Patricia Morris (past president of MIPA, Minnesota Independent Publishers Association,) and Phyllis Moore, all author-friends who have so unselfishly shared their wisdom and experience of the writing and publishing world with me. I couldn't have done this without each one of you!

I want to especially thank Nancy Schumacher and her brilliant team at Mélange Books who were my midwives and doulas throughout the birthing of my books.

Special thanks go to Sister Kristine Haugan, OCDH, who is one of my most supportive fans and beta reader. Nothing gets past you, Sister, does it?

Of course, I can't end without expressing my eternal gratitude to my dearest husband of 47 years, David, and my children, Abraham, Isaac, Ruth, Rachel, and Hannah Rose for their undying love, encouragement and support no matter how *ferhoodled* their *mamm's* latest creation appears to be.

About the Author

Midwife-turned-author, Stephanie Schwartz seems to swim seamlessly through cultures, religions, superstitions, raw fear and ecstasy to the first breath of a new baby. She knows how birth works and invites her readers to join her, taking us on a tour to the innermost workings of another world while giving us a rare, intimate glimpse into her daily life. She has five children scattered around the world, grandchildren, and over a thousand babies she calls her own. After writing three books on birth, (published under her married name, Sorensen) and then retiring as a midwife, began her foray into fiction. Thanks to the Pandemic she was able to produce the four novels in the Amish Nurse Series.

facebook.com/authorstephanieschwartz

newamishromance@yahoo.com

Also by Stephanie Schwartz

The Amish Nurse Series

Worry Ends Where Faith Begins

Time Will Tell

Playing on the Outhouse Roof

The Pearl of Great Price

The Amish Veronica Series

Wherever You Go There You Are

You Have Ravished My Heart

Merry Amish Christmas

Ephram's Quest for a Wife (Coming 2025)